EMERGENCY CALL

by

Elizabeth Harrison

Dales Large Print Books
Long Preston, North Yorkshire,
BD23 4ND, England.

British Library Cataloguing in Publication Data.

Harrison, Elizabeth
    Emergency call.

    A catalogue record of this book is
    available from the British Library

    ISBN   978-1-84262-731-0 pbk

First published in Great Britain in 1970 by
Hurst & Blackett Ltd.

Published in Large Print 2010 by arrangement with
Watson, Little Ltd.

Dales Large Print is an imprint of Library Magna Books Ltd.

Printed and bound in Great Britain by
T.J. (International) Ltd., Cornwall, PL28 8RW

CONTENTS

CHAPTER ONE

Emergency Call

The time was two in the morning, and telephones were ringing all over North London.

Richard Collingham turned over in bed and reached for the phone on the second ring. He was a surgeon, and night calls were a commonplace to him. Hardly conscious, he held the telephone and said 'Collingham' alertly. He sounded wide awake and ready for action, and by the time the telephone began quacking he was. The bedside light was on, and he held his note pad and pencil ready.

'Good morning, sir. Sorry to disturb you.'

As he had expected, the voice was that of Matthews, the night porter at the Central London Hospital.

'Can't be helped, Matthews. What is it this time?'

'This is a bad one, I'm afraid, sir.'

Richard Collingham stiffened. Unheard of for the experienced Matthews to call any road accident or surgical emergency a bad

7

one. To rate as bad in his eyes, the emergency would need to be a major disaster.

'A rail accident on the line into Euston. We're preparing for a hundred casualties. The accident flying squad will be on their way as soon as you are, Mr Collingham. They're waiting for the plasma now – otherwise they're ready to leave.'

Euston. That made the Central London the chief receiving hospital. Beds in the corridors. All staff recalled to duty.

Matthews was giving him directions. Richard wrote them down, repeated them, rang off, threw off his pyjamas (Libby found them on the floor later that morning) and climbed into his sailing gear. This would be practical, he had decided, for clambering about over a rail accident. Libby had not stirred. Years ago she had become accustomed to night calls as he. The telephone woke him, but she slept on. A child's cry alerted her at once, while he never moved. She was used, too, to waking in the morning to find him missing. She would go ahead with the children's breakfast and continue with her routine unruffled, until either he walked hungrily into the house or rang to tell her where he was and when he would be back. Today would be different, but neither of them knew that yet.

Wearing his shabby old jeans, polo-necked sweater and anorak, his dark hair ruffled, he left the bedroom and despite his weight – he was a big man of over six foot with the broad shoulders of a rugby forward – ran lightly down the old Victorian staircase.

At the foot of the stairs, just in time, he took a flying leap into the air, and managed to avoid falling over Heather's tricycle, left where she had been strictly forbidden to put it, nudging the bottom step.

He banged the front door behind him, started the car, and drove through the tangle of streets between Camden Town and Chalk Farm. He knew his derelict neighbourhood, his own home ground. When he had been appointed Resident Surgical Officer at the Central, he and Libby had decided to live in Camden Town so that he could see something of his family between operations. Now he had an appointment on the staff, on Sandy Drummond's firm. He was, as Libby assured him with a gleam in her eyes, a rising young surgeon. He had hugged her. 'Rising young surgeon,' he had agreed, 'with exceptionally beautiful wife.' For Libby was lovely, everyone at the Central agreed on that. Her black hair was drawn usually into a chignon low on her neck, and framed the oval of her face. A transparent skin and a serene forehead above deepset green eyes gave her tranquillity – though in fact Libby was not in the least tranquil. No one but she suspected this, or knew how much she depended on the support she received from the practical, unimaginative Richard.

On that particular occasion, though, her wide mouth had broken into the smile Richard alone could draw from her, a smile for him only, affectionate, humorous, with a love and devotion in its depths that were reflected in her eyes. Sometimes he felt that he drew his very existence from its radiance. He had never grown used to it – each time she took his breath away. Now she only said 'and three exceptionally wicked children. Better concentrate on the rising young surgeon, I think.'

Usually he did so, and this morning he could not prevent himself, as he drove to the scene of the crash, from experiencing the exhilaration he always knew at the approach of a difficult operation or an assignment that might have daunted others. Richard Collingham thrived on the demands made by his job. He would reach the scene of this disaster and there would be action, decisions to be taken, challenge. He had, justifiably, every confidence in himself.

There was a police barrier across the road. He stuck his head out of the window and explained his business. The policeman on the barrier summoned his colleague at the roadside, who wore a crash helmet and a walkie-talkie. He spoke into it, listened, and then turned to Richard.

'Straight down the road here, sir, and then turn left and carry on. They're sending a motorcyclist to meet you and lead you in. He'll pick you up down there.'

Richard grinned. 'That's the stuff,' he said, and let in the clutch. As he turned left at the end of the road the motorcyclist passed him, swept round in a turn, came up alongside and gave him a thumbs-up gesture, and went into the lead.

They swept unimpeded up to a road below the embankment. Here there were already ambulances, fire engines, police cars lined up. Blue lights were flashing and sirens wailing from the neighbouring streets as reinforcements continued to arrive. Portable spot lights had already been rigged on the embankment. He climbed it, into the chaos.

There was a hiss of compressed air mixed with the shouts of rescuers and the cries and moans of the injured, a stench of burning rubber mingled with the more acrid smell of smashed batteries. Somewhere a woman was weeping steadily. Another was screaming – or maybe this was a child. There were others sounds less distinguishable and more horrifying.

Already the ambulance men were there with stretchers and blankets, there were huddled figures sitting about, sobs, and moans and shouted instructions. Railway workers were there too, heaving and jacking up the shattered coaches, calling to one another, demanding the cranes and the heavy lifting equipment. The firemen were everywhere, but there seemed, thank God, to be no fire as yet.

An hour later the scene was hardy different. Richard was dirty and preoccupied. He had worked without ceasing from the moment he had paused to take breath at the top of the embankment. He was only vaguely aware that he had been joined by others, that there were nurses, now, bending over the stretchers – straight off duty, wearing cloaks over their print dresses and with their starched caps oddly reassuring and normal in a desperate scene. He had seen his registrar, too. Michael had told him that the accident team had set up an emergency theatre down below. He had been too busy to go to inspect it, but he had sent Mike back there, to route casualties back to the Central and Sandy Drummond's team in the theatre.

There were cups of tea, he saw, and as he noticed this an ambulance man pressed one into his hand.

'Cup of char, doctor. Bet you can do with it.'

'Thanks, I can,' Richard agreed. 'Very dry.' He drank the sweet strong brew and passed the cup back to the man, though what he expected him to do with it he had no notion. The cup had roses on it. That was odd. Perhaps it had come from one of the little houses in the road below. The ambulance man confirmed his unspoken guess.

'Down below, in them houses,' he remarked as he turned to go, 'they're all up and working, and the wives are running a sort of canteen.'

'Mm-h'm.' Richard was absent-minded. Then he came to life. 'See that the injured aren't given tea before they've been examined, though,' he said sharply.

'Oh, that's all right, doc.' The man grinned, his teeth showing suddenly white in his grimy face. 'The doctor down there, he soon stopped that. Quite upset, the ladies were. Brutal, they said he was.'

'Good,' Richard said heartlessly. 'Any of these people may have to go on the operating table,' he pointed out. 'They shouldn't have a drink within two hours of it. That means now.'

'O.K., doc,' the man said cheerfully, and went off.

Richard flexed his hands thoughtfully. Back on the job. They were reaching the real damage now, where the coaches had been jack-knifed. They were at last manoeuvring the heavy rescue equipment into position, and the noise had been increased by the scream of power saws cutting into metal, and the hiss of oxyacetylene cutters with their blinding glare throwing into relief the men who used them, goggled and intent.

A man came running.

'Could you come, doctor? We can't get any further, there's this bloke pinned down – and in a lot of pain, doc. If you'd come with me, I'll show you.'

He accompanied the man to the jack-knifed coaches. They had arc lights here now, and lifting gear. There was a medley of sound, but clearly audible and distinctive above it was the screaming. From quite

14

close at hand.

'Here, in this first coach,' his guide told him. 'We can't move him, he's pinned down by the leg. Afraid you'll have to crawl in underneath all this lot. We've jacked it up as far as we can. You can just about wriggle through.'

As soon as he managed to reach the man, he saw what the trouble was. He was pinned by his leg by the full weight of the caved-in steel superstructure. Before he could be moved the leg would have to be amputated.

The first need was to give him relief from pain, but he would have to have an anaesthetic preferably a general, Richard decided, for the amputation. He gave him a shot of omnopon, and told the man who had guided him, now crouched beside him in the wreckage, to nip back quickly to the control point and bring another doctor. 'Preferably an anaesthetist,' he began, and then on second thought broke off, saying, 'No, hang on a minute.' He had seen too many bad mistakes made when verbal messages miscarried. He scribbled a note. 'Send assistant, preferably anaesthetist, for emergency amputation in coach. Urgent. Bearer will act as guide.' He tore the sheet off his prescription pad and gave it to the man, who pushed himself backwards and was gone.

The injured man was quieter, and Richard thought he might be capable of understanding what was said. He began talking reassuringly. 'Soon have you out of here, and you won't have to stand much more of this. You'll be feeling much more comfortable in a minute or two, as that injection I've given you begins to take effect – better already, eh? Then we'll give you something to send you right off, and when you come to you'll be tucked up in bed all serene.'

The man muttered something about his leg.

'I know, old man. I'm seeing to that now. Don't you worry, we'll soon have you out.' Comfortable platitudes. He hoped they were true, and continued with an automatic rumble of reassurance as he made his own arrangements – unrolling the pre-sterilized instrument kit, laying out clamps and artery forceps, scalpels, bone saws, scissors, skin sutures. He poured Cetavlon into a stainless steel bowl, opened the swab pack. Where the hell was his assistant? Better prepare the Pentothal himself.

He'd have to do a disarticulation at the knee-joint. Under these conditions the simplest method was the best. They'd have

16

to tidy it up later in the theatre. He hoped he'd be able to get enough elbow room – he could hardly reach a sitting position in the confined space. Well, he'd have to do the best he could. Fortunately, disarticulation didn't demand much in the way of strength. There was going to be a hell of a lot of blood, though, and no one to swab it. He'd have to watch for the artery under the knee. He couldn't reach underneath the leg at all. Dicey. They'd have to manage somehow. He gave the patient anti-tetanus serum and penicillin, and wished the anaesthetist would hurry. Even as the thought crossed his mind he could hear someone approaching. Good. Now they'd be able to get on.

But it wasn't good. The man whose head and shoulders appeared in the light of the torch Richard had wedged into an angle of the twisted metal was a stranger.

'You'll have to leave him and get yourself out quick,' he said urgently. 'The jacks are beginning to go into the ground. It's not safe. They're liable to slip any minute.'

'Where's the anaesthetist?' This was all that interested Richard.

'Dunno, doc. But it don't matter, because there isn't time, see? You gotta get out.'

'How much time is there?' He was coldly

alert at once, the cool calculating self that invariably came alive at moments of danger in charge now.

'Matter of five minutes, perhaps. At the most. Can't really say. The jacks aren't holding, see? They're sinking into the ground, and they might slip off the frame.'

He didn't see, but he got the message. The coach was in due course going to collapse on top of them. He must have the man out before that, anaesthetist or no anaesthetist. The man had understood, too, Richard saw. His eyes were starting with terror, though he said nothing.

'Not to worry,' Richard said cheerfully. 'We'll have you out before that.' He put the Pentothal into the vein quicker than he had ever given it in his life, and wondered how rapidly he could amputate. He remembered hearing that before the days of anaesthetics surgeons could take a leg off in a couple of minutes, and he wished fervently that he had not been trained in a more deliberate school. During the battle of Trafalgar, he had once read, astounded, a surgeon had amputated a leg in fifty seconds. A record that he could not hope to emulate. The impulse to hack wildly left him almost before it had come, and he began calmly, talking to the workman at the same time, who was protesting.

'There's going to be a lot of blood, and I'll have to watch for the arteries. Get back outside, and whistle up the stretcher bearers ready to rush him down to the clearing station.' The man, muttering indistinguishably, pushed himself backwards and disappeared from sight.

The torch wasn't giving enough light to work by. Where was that chap? He'd have to hold it. Why didn't he hurry?

For the first time it occurred to him that perhaps he wouldn't risk coming back.

He was right.

But someone came.

There was a sound of grumbling and heaving, and a big ponderous sort of fellow appeared.

'Good. Hold the torch for me.'

'Look, doctor, you've got to get out. We can't count on them jacks holdin', and that's a fact. I'm the foreman, see, and I'm tellin' you straight, you've got to get out fast, or it'll be curtains.'

'Shut up and hold the torch.'

It wasn't that he didn't understand. Nor that he took any conscious decision to save the injured man regardless of risk. Simply he had a job to do, and he was doing it. If he had had time to reason, he might have decided that to leave an injured man to his fate was unthinkable. But in fact he didn't reason. He concentrated on performing the amputation as swiftly and efficiently as he could. He had no time for side issues.

The foreman, surprisingly, shut up and held the torch.

Richard cut through the muscle above the knee to free the knee-cap, and straight through the knee-joint. He pulled the thigh down towards him, felt the pulsing artery and put forceps on. Now a last quick cut.

'Right,' he said to the foreman, who was still holding the torch steadily, though his face was covered in sweat, and green even in shadow. 'Give me the torch now. You pull him out as quick as you can. But mind those forceps don't slip. They're clamping a big artery – if they come off he'll be dead inside sixty seconds, so watch it.'

The foreman began to heave, saying as he did so, 'Get after me as quick as you can, doc. I don't like the sound of it. This lot's gonna slip any minute now.'

Now that Richard had time to notice, he didn't like the sound of it either. There were ominous shiftings, some creaking and tear-ing, and there was a lot of yelling going on too. But the foreman himself was making quite a row as he dragged the unconscious man back with him, and Richard could not distinguish one set of sounds from another. He swung round to push himself after them under the girders blocking his way to safety, and ducked his head as he rolled over and began to inch forward. He at least could go out head first. Quicker.

But not quick enough.

A thunderous rushing grew and surrounded him. He knew exactly what it was. The whole damn lot was coming down on top of him. This was it.

Blast. He didn't want to die.

When he came to, he found to his surprise that he was still there, lying head downwards under the wreckage. He wasn't even in pain. Presently they'd come and get him, in his turn, out. He'd been lucky.

It was dark. He could see nothing. Where had that torch gone? He had only to wait and he'd be all right. He tried to feel for the torch, to have a bit of light on the situation, but he didn't seem to be able to move. Nuisance. There must be a good deal of stuff on top of him. Odd that he hadn't any pain. This had hardly begun to worry him when he heard the voices. Here they come, then.

Good for them. 'Just relax, Collingham,' he told himself. 'You're not in charge now. They are. Relax and let them get on with it.'

He must have relaxed to some purpose, because the next he knew his registrar, gowned and bloody and with his mask hanging, was bending over him and saying, 'You'll be fine. We'll take you straight back to the Central and you'll be fine.'

He grinned cheerfully at him and said, 'Sure. I'm leaving everything to you. Not my worry.' To his amazement Mike's face crumpled and he looked as though he was going to cry. But he jerked his head at the stretcher bearers, and they moved off. What was the matter with him, Richard wondered? Strain too much? Over-tired probably. He'd have to watch him, though.

But it all seemed very unimportant, and he wasn't much interested. He wondered vaguely what they'd done about his amputation, but he couldn't be bothered to ask.

They lifted him into the ambulance, and he saw a police motorcyclist standing by, talking to the driver. Then they were off, siren wailing, and, no doubt, he thought irritably, blue light flashing too. In addition, though this was unsuspected by him, a police motorcyclist leading them through, right to the forecourt of the Central.

In the forecourt the reporters and television newsman appreciated the entry, and came up at once to check on the ambulance and its occupant. The driver told them the truth. 'Mr Collingham,' he said. 'One of the surgeons here. Injured attending to a victim of the rail crash. They warned him, but he was operating, in one of the crashed coaches – took a leg off, they say. He wouldn't listen when they told him to get out, and the lot fell on him.'

Here was a front page story.

'Train crash latest – train crash latest. Leading surgeon badly injured.' It made the early editions of the evening papers, and was all over London by lunch time.

Long before this Richard was in the theatre, and Libby, pale and anxious, had been photographed hurrying into the hospital, accompanied by Paul Collingham, Richard's elder brother, who seldom put himself out for anyone, but who had gone so far, this morning, as to drive out to Camden Town and fetch Libby. He took her arm now firmly, and pushed past the reporters and cameramen, muttering, 'No news, no news,' and into the main hall.

The place was a shambles – though an

organized shambles. Every member of the staff of the Central was on duty, together with nurses and doctors drafted in from other hospitals. There were casualties who had recovered sufficiently to go home and who were waiting for their relatives to collect them, while other relatives waited anxiously for news. Tea and buns were being dispensed in the midst of this.

Paul pushed Libby through the lot, and up the stairs. 'No use waiting for the lift,' he said briefly. 'Now, I'm going to take you to the ward. He's going into the side room there as soon as they're through with him in the theatre, and you can wait there.' He plodded at her side up the stairs. 'I'll go back to the theatre,' he explained. 'And if there's any news I'll come straight and tell you.'

'Paul. Paul, before you go. I must know you must tell me – do you think...'

'I think it's unlikely he's dying,' he said curtly. Paul had no bedside manner. He was already, at thirty-five, renowned for the lack of it. 'No, I'd be quite surprised if he died.' As usual, he appeared to see no distinction between thinking aloud and talking to anxious relatives. 'Not yet, anyway,' he added thoughtfully. 'But...' he shrugged his shoulders. 'Just have to wait and see,' he said brightly, and was gone.

Libby watched his departure indignantly. You're a big help, she thought. She knew now exactly what Richard meant when he said that a talk with Paul convinced any patient his next stop would be the mortuary.

Sandy Drummond came to see her, worried and kindly. Sandy had once been red-headed. Now he was bald, with a rusty fringe. He was plump, and had a cheerful waddle that made any ward round of his a homely occasion for patients, though his staff found it an ordeal. His appearance was the essence of confident benevolence, and everyone trusted him. Libby's heart lifted as he entered the room. He took her hands, and his gentle eyes met hers. 'Poor Libby,' he said. 'My poor dear. What a nasty time you're having. Well, we've tidied him up, and as far as we can tell there are no internal injuries. Up to a point, he's been lucky.' He paused, and wondered whether to say more.

'Up to a point?' Libby's lips were quivering, but she managed to formulate the question and look Sandy straight in the eyes. 'What point, Sandy? You must tell me.'

'There's a partial fracture of the spine, with some injury to the cord,' he said heavily. 'This may be simply compression, in which case it should be reversible. Or, of course, it may not. Impossible to tell at present. He's in spinal shock, you see.'

'So what does that mean?'

'We have to wait and see, I'm afraid, my dear. Hard going for you, but there's no alternative. Whatever happens, you've a long illness ahead of you. No getting away from it.' He sighed, and avoided her eye. 'No point in dwelling on too many possibilities,' he added.

'If the injury to the cord isn't reversible, then what, Sandy? Tell me the truth. I've got to *know*.'

'Then he could be permanently paralysed.' He saw her face break up, and went on quickly, 'But this is to go too fast. What you have to prepare yourself for, though, is a long illness, and some long term disability. You must brace yourself for that, Libby. It's going to be a long job.'

She failed to take it all in. 'As long as he's going to live,' she said. She could see no further.

'I think he'll do that. I don't think you need worry too much about that. He's tough, and fit, and his heart and lungs are in good shape. But...' he hesitated, uncertain how much to tell her, how much she could stand. 'It'll be

26

weeks,' he continued, 'before we know how much injury there is to the cord, and whether we can get him on his feet again. The next stage will be for the neurologists – plenty of those in the Collingham family, anyway, eh? He'll be in good hands there. None better.' This was generous of Sandy. He had always disliked Professor Collingham, calling him an inhuman scientist. 'He's on his way, incidentally – your father-in-law. Be here in two hours. Well, I must go back to the theatre. Work to do. This is a devil of a situation, my dear. Try to take it as easily as you can. We'll all do our best. And I'll tell you as soon as there's any more to know.'

'Yes, of course you must go back, Sandy. I shall be all right. Don't worry.'

'There's a good girl,' he said, and went.

Libby walked edgily about the empty room.

Richard was going to live, and her father-in-law was on his way. Professor Collingham (a Central man himself) had left to take up the Chair of Neuro-Physiology in Oxford.

The information that he was on his way, as he had always been at any hint of trouble, encouraged her. He would take over and see to everything. Above all, he would understand Richard's condition. His advice about treatment would be the best in the country.

He was photographed by the press on his arrival. They tried to interview him too, and invited him to appear on television. At this point his mouth twisted sardonically, in a fashion which would have been recognized by every student he had taught. It was recognized, too, by Major Havering, the House Governor, a tall, lantern-jawed man with a military moustache and a crisp manner to match. He had been waiting to meet him and escort him upstairs to Sandy in the theatre. He leapt into the fray and collared the Mincer (as Professor Collingham had always been known at the Central – a double reference both to his habit of making mincemeat of staff and students alike, and the pedantic tones in which he did it) before he could utter one of his blistering and demoralizing retorts and ruin the good press the Central had been receiving. Major Havering, while not exactly admitting to being in favour of press publicity (an admission which would have led to his being drummed out of the Central in total disgrace) could at least distinguish between good publicity and bad, which was more than the rest of them could do. He plucked the Mincer neatly from the throng of reporters and hustled him into the waiting lift and up to the theatre. Sandy was operating still. He had now been at it for nearly twelve hours, and expected to continue until late in the evening.

The House Governor returned to the hall and the newsmen. He promised them a bulletin on Richard in time for the late editions, and agreed to supply a brief biography. The dailies wanted a human interest story so that they could give a dramatic twist to the rail disaster. Here it was, ready-made and handed to them on a plate. They clamoured for more than a brief biography. Tomorrow the national press would run the Collingham story and the Central London Hospital as a lead.

Major Havering wrote a biography from his own knowledge of Richard, adding the information that he was the third generation of Collinghams to be trained by the Central, his grandfather – another Richard Collingham having been senior surgeon until his retirement just before the war.

He obtained Professor Collingham's grudging approval, had the draft retyped and photocopied, then sallied out to distribute it himself to the press.

In the papers the next morning there was an excellent photograph of Richard and

Libby, together in New York five years earlier, both looking very young and happy – this picture did more for Richard's reputation than all the details of his career. It made Libby cry.

She saw it when she arrived back home in Camden Town with her father-in-law at tea time. Both of them had spent the previous night at the hospital, and they were exhausted. There would be no sudden change in Richard's condition, everyone assured Libby. He was under heavy sedation and there was no point in sitting at his bedside 'like Patience on a monument' Professor Collingham added somewhat un-happily, but typically. He then announced, seeing himself as the essence of helpful kindness, that he would drive her home.

Now she sat in the living room at Camden Town with the tears pouring down her cheeks, staring at herself and Richard on the front page of the *Telegraph*, thrust at her by the delighted children. 'Look, look, you and Daddy, look Mummy, you and Daddy in the paper.'

Professor Collingham did not know how to deal with her at all.

Her daughter Heather, a fat child of five with straight dark hair and a precise manner, coped admirably. 'Don't be silly, Mummy,' she said kindly. 'There's nothing to cry about. She does cry when she's only pleased,' she added informatively to her grandfather, producing a grubby handkerchief from her knickers and handing it to Libby. 'Blow,' she ordered. Libby blew. 'Better now?' Heather inquired, in a voice that brooked no denial.

'Yes, thank you, darling,' Libby said in stifled tones. She was torn now between laughing and crying, and gave a strangled choke. Professor Collingham peered at her in alarm. He hoped she was not going to become hysterical.

'You can give me back my hankie,' Heather reminded her pointedly. Libby extended it, damp now as well as grubby, and Heather restored it in her knickers. 'I shall tell Julie you want a cup of tea,' she stated, and stumped purposefully downstairs to the basement kitchen. 'Julie, pot of tea for Mummy, s'il vous plait,' she demanded. She had recently launched herself into the French language with aplomb.

'Mais assurément, chérie,' Julie agreed. 'Comment va – I mean, how eez Mummee?'

'Crying,' Heather said succinctly. 'Andrew is playing with his train, and Grampa is sitting in a chair looking cross,' she added. 'But he usually does. Daddy says he can't help it.'

'And how is Daddy?'

'Oh, Daddy's at the hospital,' Heather said airily. The children were used to Richard's absences and took them for granted. Something had been said about an accident, and that Daddy had had to be admitted, whatever that might mean. But it made very little impression. After all, he seemed to be at the hospital, as usual. What was much more interesting – sensational, in fact – was that Mummy and Daddy had their photograph in the paper. They were important people. 'I suppose,' she said thoughtfully, 'he can't have seen his photograph yet.' This was a pity.

'What did Mummee sink of ze photograph?' Julie asked. She herself was as impressed by the publicity as Heather. What letters she would write home. The English were undoubtedly odd. They lived, these Collinghams, so quietly and simply, in this terrace house in what even she could see was a poor quarter. Yet clearly, it now turned out, they were a distinguished family.

When Julie took the tea in, Libby had pulled herself together, and was listening calmly to Professor Collingham's account of the various tests that were required before anyone could have the least idea of the extent of Richard's injuries. He proposed, he told her, to leave Paul to see to these, with Sandy Drummond, and to return himself in a fortnight to assess the results. Libby was reassured. Her father-in-law had unintentionally succeeded in taking the drama out of the situation. No longer a matter of life and death in an hour or two. Instead a great many tests, all very complicated, and Professor Collingham would be back in a fortnight to look at them.

'But you must prepare yourself for a long illness, my dear,' he warned her. 'Three months as the minimum, and quite possibly a good deal longer.'

Since twenty-four hours earlier Libby had been convinced Richard was dying, she took this information in her stride.

Professor Collingham rose. 'I must go back to the Central,' he said, chucking her under the chin in a precise and distinctly Edwardian manner. He was in fact very fond of his daughter-in-law. 'Look after yourself, my dear. Have a good night's rest, and don't think of going to the hospital until tomorrow.'

At the time Libby accepted what he said.

But when she found herself alone in her bedroom that night, and knew Richard to be lying in the small side ward at the Central, solitary – here she was wrong. The little room was more like Piccadilly Circus in the rush hour – abandoned to the care of others, while she comfortably rested in their familiar bedroom, lifting not a finger, she felt selfish and neglectful, and was torn by an agony of separation. No hope of sleep for her, she paced about the room in despair. She should go to Richard. What did it matter if he was conscious or not? Her place was at his side. She would dress again and go to him.

Professor Collingham had told her not to. Paul had reinforced these instructions, telephoning during the evening with a bulletin from the ward, and Sandy Drummond had rung her from his home in Dulwich and ordered her not to stir until he had seen Richard in the morning. He would ring her then, he promised, and tell her what she should do. He alone of them had asked her if she had any sleeping tablets.

'Oh yes,' she said vaguely. 'There are some Soneryl, I think, in the cupboard.'

'Take two when you go to bed,' Sandy said firmly.

She had done nothing. She had thought

she was so tired – she had not slept for thirty-six hours – that she could not fail to sleep the moment she had the opportunity. But she had been wrong. She was alert now, wide awake, on edge. She could not bear to sit down even, but walked with little quick steps about the room.

The bedside telephone rang. She flew to it. Richard was dying. In spite of all they had said he was dying, and they were ringing to tell her so. She picked up the receiver. She was shaking.

Sandy's steady voice came on the line.

'Oh, Sandy, how – what…?'

'Richard's quite comfortable, my dear idiot. I told you he would be, and he is.'

Even in her misery, Libby experienced a flash of ironic humour. Hospitals had such an odd notion of what the word comfortable signified. In their phraseology it almost certainly meant extremely uncomfortable, but drugged sufficiently not to be in agony, and not in immediate danger of death. The word to beware of, she knew, was poorly. This meant moribund.

'I'm ringing you,' Sandy was explaining, 'because I wanted to make sure you were doing what I told you and taking those tablets.' And because, though this he did not say, neither of those two top neurologists in your family would dream of seeing you into bed with a hot drink and a sedative, though the most run-of-the-mill general practitioner would think of it. Sandy had no opinion of any of the Collinghams except Richard.

'Oh well, actually I...' Libby floundered guiltily.

'I knew it,' Sandy roared down the telephone. 'I knew it. You thought you needn't bother. You've got to look after yourself, my dear, and be very sensible.' After all, no one else in that family is capable of it, he thought furiously. 'Now, go into the bathroom or wherever you keep the things, and fetch two Soneryl.'

'Richard's study,' Libby said accurately.

'Go and get them, and then come back. I shall hold on.'

Libby trod dutifully along the passage to Richard's study and did as Sandy told her. She came back and picked up the telephone. 'Yes,' she said flatly.

'Where are they?'

'In my hand.'

'How many?'

'Two. I thought you said...'

'Yes, yes, all right, duckie.' Sandy was blaming himself. He had had a hard thirty-six hours, but he ought to have gone to Camden Town to see Libby before going home. Where was that damned father-in-law of hers? Gone back to Oxford, blast him. And Paul was useless. 'What did you do with the bottle?' he inquired fussily. To hell with this long-range stuff. He should have been there with the girl.

'Put it back in the cupboard,' Libby said, surprised.

'And then?'

'Then?'

Oh, damn the girl. 'After you'd put the bottle in the cupboard, what did you do? Is there a key or anything?'

'Oh yes. I locked it, of course, and put the key back on the top of the cupboard. That's where we keep it, because of the children, you see.'

'Good, good. Now, have you a hot drink?'

'No, no, I didn't bother. I didn't feel like...'

'Go down and get yourself a glass of hot milk,' Sandy ordered briskly. 'I suppose that *au pair* girl of yours has gone to bed by now? Yes, well, you go down and heat that milk, come back and go straight to bed, drink it and take the tablets. I shall ring you back in ten minutes and if you aren't doing precisely that I shall get the car out and come over to Camden Town and beat you.'

'Oh, Sandy, don't bother. I swear I'll...'

'Down them stairs, my girl. Ten minutes from *now.*' He range off. Libby plodded obediently downstairs, heated milk, poured it into one of the children's mugs, and climbed methodically up again. En route she spotted the *Telegraph* on the hall table and collected it, with some faint hope that to take the photograph to bed with her would make it less lonely there.

In the bedroom she climbed into the big empty bed, and almost immediately the telephone rang. 'Hello, Sandy, I've done what you said. Yes. Yes, I'm in bed and I've got the milk. Yes, I'll take the tablets. Thank you, Sandy, it was nice of you to ring. Good night.' She put the telephone back and picked up the milk. How kind Sandy was. Richard always said, 'Sandy's all right. When there's a crisis he's a tower of strength. Between times he can be a bit of a devil, of course. But he has reason, poor old Sandy. Fundamentally he's all right.' From Richard this was praise.

Absently she picked up the *Telegraph* and studied the photograph of herself and Richard while she drank the milk. She remembered the day so well. She had flown out to New York to meet Richard. She could feel the thrill again as though it had been yesterday. She had gone there to join him after the single-handed transatlantic race, and they had sailed *Nocturne* – their five-ton sloop, twenty-five feet in length, one of the Vertues built at the Cheoy Lee Shipyard in Hong Kong – back to England together. They were already tried and trusted companions, and to be alone in a small boat in mid-Atlantic was to become almost one person at last. The existence was hard at times, cold, wet and frightening, and idyllic at others, with a steady sun on a wide blue sea. They sailed alone on an ocean of discovery, shared their thoughts, emotions, sensations, loved with no interruption from the world, lived by their own timetable as one long day succeeded another. It was, they later decided, their second honeymoon.

Were they ever to be together again like that? Libby dared not face the answer. But the Soneryl did its work, and she drifted into sleep, clutching the paper.

CHAPTER TWO

Richard

A month later, Richard still lay in the side-room off what had been his own ward at the Central. He swore to himself constantly, shifted his shoulders irritably. They were all he could move. What was left of his useless body lay there unresponsive. Unresponsive, that was, to his wishes, though it answered well enough to the desires of others. He felt like a laboratory animal.

They came in, stood at the foot of his bed, chatting. Then one of them would draw a Yale key along the sole of his foot. His body responded to that all right. They commented on this fact. He had done so often enough himself. He had never imagined it felt like this to be on the receiving end.

Then they might tell him to close his eyes. They stuck pins into him. 'Can you feel that?… That?… That? M-mm. Interesting.'

He hated them all. Sandy, his brother Paul, the registrars, the physiotherapists, the nurses. The professor of medicine, the professor of surgery who made occasional appearances. One minute they manipulated him as though he were a piece of fascinating machinery, which they had by good fortune acquired at a bargain price. Then, as soon as he had managed to take this, they switched. They were back in the room with a colleague, regarding him with solemn pitiful eyes. Eyes loaded with too much feeling, with the wrong sort of compassion. He hated them anew. No one need come in here and be sorry for him.

If anyone was going to pity him it would be himself. That was quite enough to be going on with. Enough pity, and a lifetime to indulge it.

A lifetime. Barring a bit of bad luck. Or good luck, whichever way you looked at it.

From the moment he regained consciousness on the railway line outside Euston, he had suspected the worst. He should, he thought, have been in pain then, and he wasn't. He had known it for sure when he had seen all their carefully schooled blank faces. Final confirmation had come when his father appeared, talking cheerfully about a few tests, eh, and a little time, my boy, and we must see what we can do. His father had never been known to talk cheerfully unless

41

the patent was moribund or incurable. There would have been no problem there. But he soon found he was not dying. Not death for him, but life. Or half-life, to be accurate. He had challenged Sandy, forced him to admit the truth.

'Yes,' he said bluntly. 'I'm afraid you're right. Of course, I think there's room for a great deal of improvement yet. You should get a considerable amount more sensation … muscle tone … movement.'

'Come off it, Sandy. Stop beating about the bush. Tell me the worst. Where is it?' This was what they had never let out in his hearing. Never, among all their 'interestings', 'look at that', 'try this', 'what response do we elicit if we…' Among all the jargon, all the talk over his derelict frame, they had been careful never to let out the fact he was after. 'Where is it, Sandy?' he repeated. Sandy was balancing his corpulent form back and forth from heel to toe, wearing the usual irritatingly blank expression.

'All right,' he said suddenly, letting his breath out in a rush. He came clean at last. 'It looks like a T.12 lesion. That's really not too bad at all,' he added without conviction.

Richard grinned sarcastically. 'Perfectly splendid. I could easily have ended up as a quadriplegic. As it is I'm merely going to be a paraplegic. Thanks very much.'

'Afraid so,' Sandy said miserably.

It hadn't been a shock, of course. Yet to have it put finally into words like this had removed some wavering flame of hope suppressed that at last flickered out.

No more surgery. No more sailing the Atlantic. Not much more of anything, in fact. At the best, a wheelchair life for the remainder of his days.

'Some people think you should be transferred to Stoke Mandeville,' Sandy was saying.

'Eh?' Transferred to Stoke Mandeville? What the hell? Here was where he belonged, in his own hospital.

'But your father was so outspoken about it that the plan was dropped.'

'So I should hope.'

'I don't know.' Sandy was in two minds about this. He wanted Richard to be looked after in the Central, where he belonged, as they all said. He agreed, too, since he had been trained at the Central himself, with Professor Collingham's curt rejoinder, 'There is nothing they know at Stoke Mandeville that we don't know here. This is, after all, one of the leading teaching hospitals in the country.'

Sandy had continued to argue, though he knew before he began that he hadn't a hope. 'This is the Central,' they kept repeating. That was the end of the matter.

'Apart from their experience at Stoke, and the fact that they are nursing these cases all the time…'

'I must remind you, Mr Drummond, that Central-trained nurses are second to none.'

'Of course, of course. Leaving that on one side, then, I can't help feeling Collingham would be better off in a unit with other paraplegics.'

'Why?'

Sandy hedged. He could not see how to put this. 'More encouraging for him. Less isolated. There'd be more stimulus, and it would be less depressing.'

Professor Collingham took his point with ease. 'My son is not a neurotic,' he said bitterly. They were all with him. They all disliked Sandy's implication. He had not intended to disparage Richard, but this was how his remarks had been taken. He tried to explain himself.

'My son is a Central man,' Professor Collingham continued in his coldest tones. 'We are a Central family. We've served the

Central for three generations now, as many of you may be aware. My son received his injury in the service of this hospital, and I for one should consider it a poor effort if this hospital failed to care for him. Har-rmph.'

That, not unnaturally, was the end of that.

Sandy thought the decision mistaken. The wrong decision, taken for the right reasons. They were making it, he knew, more difficult for Richard.

Certainly he was taking it badly, though this had not been apparent at first. After Sandy had given him the diagnosis he had seemed unchanged. He remained resolutely cheerful for nearly a week. Sandy knew why. He had taken that time to assimilate the blow.

The account of the rail disaster had been front-page news, and the leading story had been of Richard Collingham's heroism. 'Young surgeon defies death – saves injured man in train wreckage' the headlines had screamed. The following days the papers carried lurid accounts of what they described as 'Injured surgeon's battle for life'. Richard had read none of these stories. But he knew, as did the entire reading public, that the decision to remain had been his own. As a result he was permanently crippled. Would he take the same decision again, knowing the price to be paid? Sandy wondered.

Richard wondered, too. He hoped that he would, though on the whole he thought it unlikely. The patient whose leg he had amputated – the last piece of surgery he would ever execute – was along the corridor in the ward, recovering. He had asked to see Richard, Sandy told him.

Richard refused, vehemently.

Sandy had not pressed the point.

For over a month Richard lay on his back in his room in a towering rage. His words were civil enough, but they came out in a biting manner reminiscent of the Mincer on one of his most terrifying teaching rounds. Now he terrified them all as much as his father had ever done. For there was force behind his anger. They flinched from encountering it, though they all knew the anger was directed not at them, but at life. Its power still destroyed them.

He lay as he would lie for nearly three months, fully extended along the hospital bed, on the Sorbo packs they used at Stoke Mandeville. The nurses turned him every two hours. The physiotherapists gave him passive movements twice daily. A useless hulk. He could not accept himself.

Least of all could he accept himself in relation to Libby.

Libby who had worshipped him once, sat now at his bedside pitying him.

This was intolerable.

One thing was certain. She need not think she was going to take him home and nurse him. He had given her three children. He was damned if he was going to become the fourth, dependent and querulous. But what else was ahead of him?

He was a surgeon, and he knew too well the shifts his dilapidated body would be put to, in the years to come, to maintain life. He knew the exact effect of the impaired function that would accompany him inexorably to the grave. He flinched helplessly from the prospect of exposing himself in this way to Libby.

His brother Paul came in. He had not changed. Brisk and heartless in the past, he remained brisk and heartless now that Richard was on his back, disabled. Richard found it a relief. They quarrelled mildly, as they had done since childhood. They had always exasperated one another. But at least there was no destroying pity in Paul's eyes. As far as Paul was concerned, Richard was merely another job to be done. Paul not only did not display, he clearly felt none of the grief and distress that others knew. Richard found himself almost welcoming his visits, uncomplicated as they were by emotional overtones. He certainly enjoyed repulsing the acid little thrusts that were the normal ingredients of Paul's conversation. Mincer Junior, he was known in the Central. Like his father, his voice was thin, his diction meticulous, and his brain exceptional.

He tested Richard's reflexes, moved his legs experimentally, produced and used the inevitable pin, finally straightened and remarked, 'Umph-aah.' This was Paul's variation on Professor Collingham's throat clearing, and was less downright than his father's, more of a thin, precise assessment. 'Umph-aah. Ye-es. Spasticity is a li-ttle less trouble to you, I daresay. Yes. There is some slight progress. Umph-aah. Yes. I think we may say so. But I'm afraid it's very slow. Yes.'

'You're telling me.'

Paul's eyes shifted. He regarded Richard in a startled manner, as though for the first time he remembered he was talking to his brother. 'Umph-aah,' he said carefully, weighing his words. 'It'll all be the same in a hundred years, old boy,' he added brightly, and went out.

Richard grinned. Typical. His brother's notion of comfort amused him considerably. He knew Paul meant well by his remark, that it represented a genuine effort at sympathy. He was till grinning at the episode when his door opened, and Adam Trowbridge came in.

'What's the joke?' he demanded immediately – they had not met for two or three weeks, but his absence of any form of greeting was normal for Adam, who would drop in and out on his friends in the same way whether he had last seen them three hours or three years ago.

'Paul's just gone,' Richard explained.

'Yes, I met him in the corridor. All he needs is a monocle.'

'His contribution to my joy in living was, "It'll all be the same in a hundred years, old boy." Exit.'

Adam chuckled. 'He's a big help, as usual. How are you, anyway?'

'So-so.'

'H'm.' Adam's eyes flicked intently over Richard's face and arms, all that were visible of him. He retreated to the end of the bed and began reading the charts. Richard had known Adam almost all his life. They had been at school together, then students at the Central, then housemen, finally registrars. Adam was short, blunt-featured (and

49

bluntly spoken), with a broken nose, brilliant blue eyes, a round bumpy forehead, a smooth cap of thin blond hair, a square pugnacious chin, and a mouth that could seem as blunt and heartless as his words or as gentle and vulnerable as a child's. Then it seemed, surprisingly, that he could be easily hurt, almost destroyed. He had been.

He had once been Sandy Drummond's registrar, and a brilliant future – much more striking than Richard's was expected to be – had been forecast for him. But he had thrown it away. He had fallen hopelessly in love with Sandy's young wife, Elspeth, a fascinating girl of wild rose beauty. Adam had been too inexperienced to see that she was both shallow and heartless. He had loved her, had planned to marry her, had been prepared to sacrifice everything for her. When she discovered that divorce and remarriage to Adam meant the ruin of his career (a possibility that had not crossed what passed for her mind until the reality was almost upon them both) she had been horrified. No consultant post at the Central for Adam, no comfortable life in London for her – this was unthinkable. She decided, belatedly, to play safe and remain with her husband. She had thrown Adam over. Not content with this, she had confessed all to Sandy, who until then had been almost the only human being in the Central unaware of what was going on. He had trusted Elspeth completely. And Adam too.

Adam had resigned, and Richard was offered the post Adam had been expected to take, that of Resident Surgical Officer.

They had remained, unalterably, friends, and since Richard's injury Adam had been travelling up to see him regularly from Halchester, the cathedral city on the coast where he had finally found a job. The bad days were behind him now. He had settled at St Mark's, Halchester, done well, and was a consultant there at last, running a new accident unit. He had married a local girl, Catherine Halford of Halford Place. Adam had remade his life.

He appeared to expect Richard to do the same without delay. This increased Richard's anger, and Adam's visits, beginning amicably, were apt to end with the two of them glaring furiously at one another. Richard enjoyed a good fight with Adam, who looked at him with sparks in his eyes and a jutting chin. This was not only invigorating, but almost a comfort after the pity he met from the rest of them. His visits set Richard up. A good satisfying encounter. No soft looks. Instead, blazing blue eyes and the mouth that knew how to be gentle set into a thin hard line.

Richard's bad temper was not entirely due to unhappiness. He was lost because he had been physically vigorous always, and had discharged any aggression in bodily action. Now it was eating away at him, burning fiercely in heart and mind.

Adam talked to Sandy about the problem. The two of them met in the corridor outside Richard's room. Adam conscious only of Richard's need, forgetting the terms on which he and Sandy had parted five years before, said casually, 'Oh, Sandy, there you are. I wanted to have a word with you. Have you a minute?' He had then taken in Sandy's entourage of registrar, houseman, Sister Paré, students, visiting Americans and Indians, and apologized.

At the Central they had been anticipating this encounter. The story of how Sandy had once wrecked Adam Trowbridge's career had been resuscitated for the benefit of those too junior to have experienced it at first hand, and Adam, on his visits to Richard, pointed out – not as a visiting celebrity exactly, more as a notorious character from beyond the pale. The assembled ward round was agog now to see their first meeting and its outcome. Alarming and delightful possibilities sprang to mind.

'In sister's office,' Sandy said. 'In just one moment. Sister, may I? Thank you so much.' He began shaking hands firmly with his distinguished visitors, said, 'Later, later,' to his hovering houseman, informed the visitors in a body that Mr Illingworth would show them tomorrow's list, and pushed his way past them all into Sister Paré's office, followed by Adam.

'Shut the door,' he said briefly. These were the last words the expectant staff were to hear, and they regarded them as promising fireworks. All of them had been demolished by Sandy on occasion, and since he, unlike many of the senior staff, normally took no pleasure in performing this operation in public, the preliminary 'shut the door' was accepted as ominous. Sandy could be irritable and tetchy with his staff, but Adam was the only member of it he had consistently and publicly humiliated. He knew this, and he had been ashamed of it for many years past.

'Sit down,' he said brusquely. 'Richard. You've been seeing him. Have you spoken to his father about him—'

'Not recently,' Adam said uncomfortably. He had remembered that he ought to have been embarrassed to meet Sandy, and certainly should have hesitated before barging into the middle of his ward round with demands for a talk. However, they were in the middle of the conversation now, so if Sandy was wearing it, he could. His lips twitched involuntarily, as he suddenly understood the significance of the silence and the expectant faces outside. Food for the grapevine. He put all this aside and settled down to listen to Sandy talking about Richard.

'As a matter of fact, I think he would have been better at Stoke Mandeville.'

'At Stoke Mandeville?' This was a new idea to Adam. 'But – but he's a Central man, and – and surely we can...' he stumbled. He could not justifiably say 'we' these days. But Sandy appeared not to notice.

'Everyone would agree with you. Particularly Professor Collingham. I'm not sure they're right, because for one thing they have a great deal of very specialized experience at Stoke, and for another I think it would be better for him psychologically there. Here he's stuck in the middle of all of us, and we're leading the life he used to lead. It's holding him in the past, and delaying his recovery, I think.'

'There's a lot in that. It must make it extraordinarily difficult.'

'He's extremely uncooperative, you know,' Sandy paused. Uncooperative was a very rude word when used of patients, and he thought Adam might resent it on Richard's behalf.

He agreed, though. 'I know,' he said easily. 'Every time I come to see him he has a row with me. Just had one now. He hates the sight of everyone of us.' He shrugged. 'Well, can you blame him?'

'No. But you see why I think he might have been better at Stoke. However, that's a dead duck.'

'"Surely the waters of Abana and Pharpar are better by far than the waters of Babylon?"'

'That's it exactly. Professor Collingham for one was most offended. I've done what I can, though. Sister and I took a day off and drove over to Stoke and went through the place with a small toothcomb. We're not proud. I talked to everyone I could lay hands on, and so did Sister.'

Adam was impressed.

'We came back with a good many nuggets of information, which we've quietly incorporated into our way of life here.'

'The best of both worlds, probably, he has now.'

Sandy sighed. 'I'd like to think so, but I doubt it. I don't think this place is at all good for him. However, there's about another month to go before we can let him off his back. That's when the struggle will begin. In the meantime I've persuaded two of the physios to go out to Stoke for the day. They were very shocked at the idea, but they've come back full of enthusiasm and plans, I'm glad to say.'

'You make me feel I ought to make time to have a look round there myself,' Adam said. 'I spend half my time on the telephone trying to find jobs for teenagers who've crashed their motor bikes and disabled themselves for life. But the trouble is I'm an infant in the field of rehabilitation myself.'

Adam had always spent half his time on the telephone. He was capable – Sandy had missed this attribute ever since he had left the Central – of performing the most astonishing feats of persuasion and achievement on it. Sandy could easily imagine him stirring up the countryside for a hundred miles by his telephonic bullying. He knew an instant of bitter regret for the past. He had been fond of Adam. They could have been friends and colleagues, had it not been for Elspeth. All old history, of course. At least the boy had fallen on his feet, and appeared to be making a success of his accident unit.

'I wonder,' he said, his eyes focusing on Adam as the plan dawned, 'if we could send Richard down to you for a change, once he's off his back?'

'Seaside convalescence at St Mark's?' Adam was struck by the suggestion. 'You know, that might be just the job. I wonder if old Mincer would stand for it?'

'I've had to give in about Stoke, I'm damned if I give in twice,' Sandy said belligerently.

Adam grinned. 'Then I shall leave him to you,' he said, his eyes sparkling.

'Do that. Could you lay on St Mark's satisfactorily, do you think?'

'I'd be prepared to turn the place upside down,' Adam retorted.

Sandy knew he was entirely capable of this. The project grew on him. 'Right,' he said. 'That gives us something to work towards. Excellent. Say a month from now, we have him sitting up and in a chair. Then a month after that, down to you, eh?'

'We'll be ready.'

'Let's hope for your sake he'll be less bloody-minded than he is now.'

'Oh, he'll come round when he's ready,' Adam was unperturbed. 'I don't worry about him.'

'Then you're about the only one who doesn't,' Sandy remarked.

'Do you worry?' Adam was surprised. 'No need. The disaster is appalling, I agree. Tragic. But we have to accept it, as he does. That's what's wrong with this place, of course.' He saw this immediately. It had not struck him until now, but this was the trouble. 'You're all, not only Richard, living in the past. Too much regret and not enough planning for the future.'

'You may be right there,' Sandy agreed slowly. By God, he thought, the boy was right. It had taken Adam Trowbridge to bring the future into line for Richard Collingham. At the Central they had behaved like a collection of old men wringing their hands. 'Just wringing our hands and moaning,' he said irritably.

'Eh?'

'All we've been doing, in this fine old teaching hospital with its magnificent traditions. It takes someone like you to come along and stir us up. An old man's

58

paradise, I sometimes think, this place.'

Adam was amazed. He had great respect for the Central, and considered that his own career would remain second rate all his days simply because he had not been able to get on to the staff there.

'A breath of fresh air,' Sandy continued. 'For us and Richard. You fix it. I'll fix the pundits.'

'Right.' Adam grinned happily.

'So you don't worry about Richard?' Sandy demanded. This surprised him, but it might possibly be the correct attitude. No one knew Richard better than Adam.

'I'm sad about what's happened, of course. Who wouldn't be? And I worry rather about Libby, but not about Richard. Not fundamentally. No.'

'Why not?'

'He'll make out.'

'But will he? At the moment he's refusing to accept reality.'

'He doesn't like it. How should he? A perfectly normal reaction. When he's ready he'll deal with the situation.'

'He's making himself very unhappy. The sooner he snaps out of it, the better for him. Or it may be too late. That's what I'm afraid of.'

'When you have a hard knock like this, you need time to adjust. You know what's happened to you, but this isn't enough. You have to wait until you find you've somehow managed to accept it. Then you're ready to start again. Give him time.'

Sandy listened and was amazed again. This was not the brash young Adam he had known. Breaking with Elspeth and ruining his career had taught him this. Adam himself had forgotten when and how he had learned what he was busily putting over to Sandy. He was thinking only of Richard and how to deal with his problems. But Sandy, for the first time, felt pity for the young Adam of five years earlier, caught in a trap sprung by Elspeth. He would have liked to put the clock back and lived it all differently.

'No one can hurry this process,' Adam was saying. 'I don't think it's even right to try. Let him take it at his pace. Why should he take it at ours?'

'It's hard on those who have to watch him. Libby, for instance. Hardest of all on her.'

Adam remembered how fond Sandy had always been of Libby. 'Yes,' he said slowly. 'I've been worried about Libby. How is she taking it? I've hardly seen her recently, only spoken to her on the telephone. The trouble is, I have so little time. I find it pretty difficult to get away at all, and when I do I rush straight in here.'

Sandy frowned. 'Libby is exhausted. I don't know what to do about it. She comes in here every day to sit with Richard, and each day she looks paler and thinner, more hag-ridden, with bigger shadows under her eyes. I take one look at her, and want to pack her straight off to the south of France to lie in the sun for weeks on end. But she couldn't go, of course. She has to live through this, just as Richard does, and she has to cope with the children. Three under five is a handful at the best of times, and this is the worst of times. But' – he frowned, and his eyes were perplexed – 'the odd thing is that…' He broke off, sighed, and pressed his lips together. 'I haven't mentioned this to anyone so far,' he admitted. 'I don't quite know what to do about it. But, you know, Libby makes Richard worse. There's no getting away from it. She has a bad effect on him. You'd think she'd be a support. She's a good girl, calm and loving. Not demanding, or upsetting in any way, as far as one can see. Yet he's always on edge and far more uncooperative when she's here, or when she's just gone, than at any other time. In some way she upsets him, and I can't get to the bottom of it. Sister has noticed it too.'

'I expect, you know, that she reminds him more than anyone else of what life used to be. After all, he was always the one who wore the pants in that marriage. Very much so. Almost Victorian, occasionally, it was. He wouldn't readjust there very easily. Personally, I don't see why he should have to – but he may be afraid he must.'

'Yes. I'd wondered if it was something like that. Afraid of not being the dominating partner, so to speak.'

'It'll wear off. He always will be.'

'Oh yes, I think it's merely a phase.'

'I must get Catherine to come and have a talk to her,' Adam said confidently. Then he heard what he'd said. 'Er – um – er – I don't know if you'd – er – heard I got married.' He was bright scarlet, and Sandy, somewhat to his own surprise, had no emotion other than sympathy and a determination to put him out of his distress as soon as possible.

'Does she know Libby well?' he asked at once. 'Because if so I think it would be what she needs. She has no woman to advise her, only that young *au pair* girl – a nice enough child, but simply a child.'

'Catherine and I will come up for a long

week-end,' Adam decided. His momentary confusion was behind him after all, this was not the first time he had been thrown into confusion in Sandy's presence. It had been happening since he had been a student. He leafed through his battered diary. 'Not next week-end. Perhaps the one after, if – yes, I don't see why not.'

'Libby needs a holiday, you know,' Sandy said. 'And I can't honestly see why she shouldn't have one. It wouldn't do either of them any harm to be separated for a week or two. In any case, if we're going to move Richard down to you at St Mark's, she'll have to – the trouble is, what about the children? Libby needs a holiday from them, even more than from Richard.'

'She has this *au pair* girl. Professor Collingham has his housekeeper in Oxford. Let them look after the children. About time they took a hand.'

Sandy smiled to himself. This was recognisably Adam handling the patient's family. He was a little apt to ride roughshod, but his plans usually worked in the short term, and this was all they were concerned with on the surgical side at the Central. He wished his present registrar, young Illingworth, had half Adam's flair for family management, and even a quarter of his drive.

'I'll leave them to you, then,' he said, as he had so many times in the past. They left the office, and walked out on to the landing together. 'You'll lay it all on at St Mark's, then, and let me know, eh?' Sandy asked.

'Yes. And we'll see Libby the week-end after next, and fix her up then.' Adam raised a casual hand in farewell, and ran down the stairs. He had always been too impatient to wait for the lift.

Sister Paré materialized. 'There you are, Sister,' Sandy said at once. 'Sorry I've been monopolizing your office in this way. But to some purpose, at least. Now, what we decided is…' He put his arm affectionately round her shoulders and walked her back into the office. His registrar and houseman were left gaping and disappointed. What had all that been about?

'Yes,' Sister Paré said when he had finished. 'I think that's a good plan.' She too had been wondering what Sandy and Adam could have been discussing, and she was amused to find it had been the welfare of the Collinghams. Men, she thought. Trouble over a woman may throw them from time to time. But basically they're more interested in their jobs than in any woman. It all blows over and they're back where they started. It was a pity… She wrenched her thoughts back to the present, and added, 'I've been very worried about poor Libby Collingham. She looks as if she'll collapse at any moment. You're quite right. She needs a holiday, and there's no reason at all, as far as her husband is concerned, why she shouldn't have one. It would be a relief to both of them, I shouldn't wonder. And then she'll be fit and well when you're ready to move him down to Halchester.' She broke off, as an idea struck her. 'Halchester,' she repeated thoughtfully. 'I wonder, now. That might come in very useful.'

'What might, Sister?'

'Young Nurse Marshall comes from Halchester. She might travel down there with Mr Collingham.'

'Nurse Marshall. Do I know her?'

'Probably not. She's an agency girl, who came with the others for the rail disaster. She's stayed, because of the influenza epidemic. She's quite a good little nurse, otherwise we wouldn't have kept her. Not Central-trained, of course, but not bad at all. Quite ravishingly pretty, incidentally. Blonde and ethereal.'

'A pretty blonde, eh? Just the job. Splendid idea. Wheel her in, Sister.'

'Who to?' Sister Paré asked, with a spurt of laughter. 'You, or Mr Collingham?'

'I'm an old man, Sister,' Sandy said. He often felt it, anyway. He rose and patted her amiably on the shoulder on his way to the door.

Sister Paré (otherwise Anthea Ritchie) could not help longing that just for once he would touch her with meaning, not in the friendly absent-minded fashion he used to half the hospital and almost all his patients. She had been in love with Sandy for twenty years, since he had been a houseman and she a staff nurse on this very ward. She had thought herself heartbroken when he had married Elspeth. She had been wrong, of course. Her heart had not broken, and she had enjoyed her twenty years. But the failure of Sandy's marriage, and the gossip in the hospital about it, twisted her unbroken heart in a vice.

She shrugged all this away, and sent for Nurse Marshall.

CHAPTER THREE

Victoria and Libby

Victoria Marshall could hardly believe her luck when Sister told her she was to go the side-ward and nurse Mr Collingham. She would be the envy of all her friends.

Victoria had not nursed in a London teaching hospital until she was drafted in to the Central London Hospital in the emergency after the Euston rail disaster. The experience itself thrilled her, and then after a week, she found herself on Paré Ward, where Richard Collingham's beds had been, and where he himself was under treatment. She saw his brother, Mincer Junior as they called him, going in daily to see Richard, and his beautiful wife, so dark and tragic, quietly coming and going. Mr Drummond was always perfectly sweet to her, they all agreed, he put himself out for Libby Collingham as he would for no one else.

They said Richard Collingham was impossible to deal with now. Formerly so good-humoured, even-tempered, he was abrupt and disagreeable, and as sardonic as his brother and father, by-words in the hospital. Victoria had never seen Professor Collingham, and on the evening after Sister Paré had told her she was to move she went up to the nurses' home – on the excuse of helping Jennifer Darbyshire with the dress she was making – to glean all the additional information she could about the Collinghams.

Jennifer knew everyone, of course. She had not only trained at the Central, but was the daughter of a consultant there.

'The Collinghams?' she queried, looking up from the hem she was pinning.

'Yes. Of course I know what the papers said. I just wanted to know more about them all. There was a picture of Richard Collingham and his wife in New York, for instance, and it said something about a transatlantic race. And who exactly is Professor Collingham? I know he's a neurologist, but where? He's not on the staff here, is he?'

'No, but he used to be. And he trained here. He's an absolute brute, and brilliant as they come. I used to quake if I so much as passed him in the corridor. He had a nasty cold eye, and an even colder voice, and they say he liquidated more housemen than any other surgeon in London. Thank heaven he gave up clinical practice for research, and went to Oxford. What a relief, I can't tell you. He's fearfully grand, with strings of letters after his name. Fellow of the Royal Society, and all that guff. Paul is his eldest son, nearly as clever – but not quite, they say – and a frightful old misery. Richard used to be the only human member of the family. He was famous outside the hospital, too, but not in the same field as Dad. Rugby and yachting. He and Adam Trowbridge were Olympic Gold Medallists, believe it or not. They were tremendous friends, too; until Adam was thrown out for having an affair with Sandy Drummond's wife.'

'He's the one,' Victoria exclaimed at once. 'He was in yesterday. Stocky and fair, with very blue eyes and a chin like a prizefighter.'

'That's him, duckie. He came to see Richard, I suppose? I wonder what he felt like, coming back here?'

'There was tremendous excitement on the ward, because he accosted Sandy Drummond at the end of his ward round, and they both disappeared into Sister's office, shut the door and didn't come out for hours on end. Everyone thought it was pistols for two and coffee for one, but when they reappeared, they were simply chatting away about some patient or other. Anticlimax. Everyone was very dashed.'

'How madly exciting. I wish I'd been there. D'you mean to say he and Sandy were simply talking away as if nothing had happened? What a turn-up for the book.'

'You wouldn't think there'd ever been a cross word. Even Sister admitted she was shaken.'

'I must say, you do see life on Paré. Look, I've pinned it.' She stood up and clambered into the minidress, pirouetted dubiously, squinting at the mirror. 'Do you think it's all right?'

'Depends where you want to wear it,' Victoria said cautiously.

'Actually, at Deborah's party tomorrow night.'

'Oh yes, it'll be perfect. As long as you weren't thinking of wearing it at home to Sunday lunch or anything like that.'

'Heavens, no. Dad would throw a fit.'

'So would mine,' Victoria agreed with a spurt of laughter, though in fact her father seldom opposed her, but spoilt her delightedly – had, her sister maintained with some truth, done his best to ruin her. He asserted that her métier in life was to live at home with him and be decorative. This she undoubtedly was. But at eighteen she had been filled with the not uncommon urge to make a life for herself, coupled with a fervent longing to serve humanity. Charity begins at home, her father suggested hopefully, but on this occasion he lost the battle.

But he was a skilful businessman, expert in hard bargaining, and he soon retrieved the situation. To please him Victoria gave up her plan to nurse in London (he displayed his pleasure by augmenting her allowance and buying her a Triumph Herald convertible). Victoria went to St Mark's, Halchester, and here, after some vicissitudes, she had eventually taken her finals and become state registered. Afterwards she enjoyed a long holiday at home – breakfast in bed, new clothes by the crateful, barbecues on the shore for her friends left behind at St Mark's slaving, a new car, and a trip to Malta – then, recuperated and ready for action, and estranged from her latest boy friend, she looked round for new worlds to conquer. She toyed with the possibility of joining Queen Alexandra's Royal Army Nursing Corps and travelling. They wore those charming little red caps, too. Or she might volunteer for a mission hospital in Africa or India. Or even go to Vietnam?

These ideas came to nothing. When it came to the crunch, she was afraid to go so far, afraid to leave her own secure background and her devoted father – besotted would be a better word, some of her friends considered. Finally she settled on the London nursing agency. They paid well, and she would not be tied down. She could have a flat in London, and take a holiday when she felt like it. Go to Bermuda with Daddy, for instance. He, predictably, increased her allowance again, to cover the rent of what could reasonably be described as a luxury flat.

Both Victoria Marshall and Jennifer Darbyshire were privileged, but they were also, even if only spasmodically, hardworking. Meeting at the Central, they quickly established an undemanding friendship, finding that they had problems in common that their impecunious contemporaries never suspected.

'I'll hem it then,' Jennifer said now, wriggling cautiously out of the scanty slip of a frock. 'Where had we got to?'

'Adam Trowbridge.'

'Oh yes. Well, he's working at some place out in the wilds.' At the Central, 'out in the wilds' could mean any hospital more than twenty miles from Charing Cross, where outer darkness was assumed to reign.

'St Mark's, Halchester,' Victoria said promptly. 'He was R.S.O. there when I trained. But I never knew all this about him. I wish I had. Not that he ever took the faintest notice of me.'

'Nor me,' Jennifer agreed. She bit off some cotton and threaded her needle thoughtfully. 'Such a pity,' she added. 'I've always felt I could rather go for him. Just my type.'

'Too bloody-minded for me, thank you,' Victoria retorted at once. 'You can have him. You'd better make that skirt an inch or two shorter and then trying hovering on the stairs outside Paré showing your legs and flashing your eyelashes.'

'Why? Do you think he'll come often?'

'I've seen him a couple of times. I'd better do an investigation into his timetable and let you know.'

'Then I'll come along and do my stuff. He had no time for anyone except that ghastly Elspeth Drummond before, but I always thought he was rather gorgeous. I was still at school though, and for ages I couldn't find out what had happened. Not in front of the chee-ild, my dear. I got it out of my mother in the end, though. I must say, you are a lucky devil, getting right into the middle of it all. I think it's most unfair, when you didn't even train here.'

'You haven't told me yet about Richard Collingham himself – apart from him being an Olympic Gold Medallist. What in?'

'Sailing. He and Adam never did anything else in their spare time all summer. Rugby in the winter. They both played for the hospital, and the university, and Richard was reserve for England. Hence his great broad shoulders. Dad says he's going to need his great broad shoulders now.'

'Why on earth?'

'Strength. Muscle power. Once he decides to come out of his gloom and pick up the pieces of his life, it'll be his shoulder muscles that he'll depend on. Now I must press this thing. Are you coming, or are you going home?'

'I think I'll go home. Have an early night for once. Got to be at my best tomorrow.'

'I do see your point,' Jennifer agreed. She sailed off to the ironing room, leaving Victoria to float ecstatically downstairs and hail a taxi. She could hardly wait for tomorrow. This was the stuff of her dreams, at last.

In the morning she did her hair with as much concentration as if she had been launching a space ship. She back-combed it to hold her cap at exactly the right angle, and pinned it up three times before she was satisfied with the result. She made up her eyes with the same meticulous precision, drew in her state-registered belt another inch, patted her flat tummy a little smugly, and addressed her image in the mirror. 'Go in and win,' she said.

Libby was glad to see her. She thought this pretty blonde who seemed gentle and kind, with a charming soft voice, would be good for Richard. She only hoped he would not inspire so much terror in her, treat her so abominably, that she refused to nurse him, asked to be moved back on to the ward. This was the only danger she saw.

Libby knew exactly what was wrong with Richard. He was angry with life, because this had happened to him, and he took out his anger on whoever was around, and especially on anyone who dared to suggest he should plan for the future. This, she knew, was why he almost seemed to dislike her. He felt the pressure of her longing that he should do just this, and was aware of her suffering because he could not. It put him into a raging fury with her. He tried to control it, but she was always conscious of it like a dark cloud round him. It defeated her. She could read him as easily as she could read the children when they were fractious, but this was no help. She shrivelled to nothing when she felt his anger.

Pain accompanied her throughout her day, and threatened to tear her apart each time she entered his room and saw him lying there helpless, inert, except for the rage which devoured him. The pain was destroying her.

It was a pain shared by the medical and nursing staff. They had all, after all, known him when he had been active and busy, working in the wards, clinics and theatres. To see him as he was now hurt them. They could not accept what life had done to him any more than Libby could.

Their anguished pity made matters more difficult for Richard. Sandy had been right in his first judgement. Richard would have been better off at Stoke Mandeville, away from his sorrowing colleagues, whose pain impeded his own struggle to adjust. Each day he saw the magnitude of his loss reflected in their eyes as they came and went about his bed. He rejected it and them. He had to. Any other response would have meant defeat, acceptance of a second-class life.

The pain was worst for Libby, and he

rejected her awareness of the change in him most of all. If he saw himself through her eyes he would be defeated finally. What she saw was that Richard, who had been so strong and active, whose body she had depended on and loved, was frail now. He had lost 42 pounds, his face which in the past had shown his strenuous outdoor life was pale and new lines had altered it, she sometimes thought, almost beyond recognition. Worst of all, his body was no longer his friend but his enemy. All this was more than Libby could bear. She tried to control herself, and Richard, she hoped, never suspected what she was feeling. She never confided in him. She thought it her duty to keep her troubles to herself. He had enough of his own. She never asked for his support.

He recognized this, and it unmanned him. He was useless. He had had a purpose in life, at work and at home. All gone.

Libby told him nothing of her pain or her loneliness – he longed to hear that she found it difficult to manage without him – and certainly nothing of her daily household worries.

These were not negligible. Her *au pair* girl, Julie, was kind to the children and cheerful, but she was also forgetful and impulsive. She was only eighteen, and she felt deeply

77

for Libby. She longed to be able to help her in her loneliness, which Julie recognized at once. But her longing failed to prevent her from forgetting to stoke the boiler, forgetting to put the casserole in the oven or do the potatoes for lunch. She was too young to guess that to have the petty details of household management taken off her shoulders would be more help to Libby than the most subtle intuitive sympathy.

Libby had had more than enough of emotion at present. She rejected additional offers of it as firmly as Richard would have done.

At home she was preoccupied. Her mornings were devoted to starting the day off satisfactorily for the three children and getting herself out of the house and along to the Central to Richard. Her afternoons, when Julie was at her classes, to doing the shopping, taking the children for their walk, and giving them their tea. She spent alternate evenings either at the Central with Richard or at home with the children if Julie was out. For Julie, she had little attention to spare and less affection. She should, she reminded herself occasionally, try to take some interest in her life, in her hopes and fears, even if she was unable to offer her a more stimulating time. But she was exhausted by the daily round, by her anguish for Richard, and by the responsibility of running her house and family alone. She had always been dependent on Richard's support, and doing without it was a constant struggle.

Except at the hospital, she saw few adults, for there was no opportunity – even if she had wished to do so – to go out and meet friends, and she was too tired to invite them in. Hardly anyone came to call on her. In the early days they had done so, had tried to rally round. But they found that Libby was seldom at home. When she was, she was obviously rushing to go to the hospital or the shops, and they soon felt their well-meant visits to be more of an intrusion and a nuisance than the support they had intended. Only Sandy Drummond continued to drop in at all hours. He never stayed long, simply took a cup of tea or coffee, or a whisky, off her, according to the time of day, chatted generally, played with the children if they were still up, and then drove back to the Central. His visits, though, were a life-line. Sometimes she felt they kept her sane. This was not as dramatic an attitude as it might seem, for these days she knew herself often on the verge of hysteria.

She knew miserably that she was neglecting the children. To see them fed and clean was her limit. She saw less of them than she had ever done, and when she was with them she was too tired and despondent to respond to them. Julie, she often felt, was more use to them than she was.

If she could have told Richard of her guilt and anxiety over the children, she knew he would have scoffed. 'Don't fuss about nothing,' would have been his reply. But it would have reassured her, in a way that giving herself the same advice failed to do. In his present mood, though, she was too frightened of him to approach him, even if she had thought it fair to bother him with her own domestic worries. She wondered if perhaps this new pretty young nurse would be able to calm him. She had a tranquil beauty, and she moved about his room lightly and quietly, her grey eyes soft and her lovely mouth gentle. Even Richard in his present mood could hardly fail, Libby hoped, to be softened by her presence. She herself was almost staggered by the girl's beauty. To watch her was sheer pleasure.

If only the tension and anger left Richard, Libby thought she could begin to turn her attention to the children again – for the baby Gavin, for instance. She never played with him for hours together as she had done with the other two when they were babies. Would he grow up suffering from this lack? Deprived?

She had, she told herself, allowed home to take second place for long enough. Especially as she appeared not to be the slightest use to Richard in any case. She must pull herself together and pick up the threads of home and children.

Easier said than done. Nothing happened. This surprised her. It was not like her. She was used to hard work, and until now she had enjoyed it. Ever since she had first met Richard (he had been a house surgeon in his pre-registration year, and she a speech therapy student doing practical training at the Central) she had been at his side. She had watched rugby in pouring rain or freezing cold, had accompanied him to Burnham-on-Crouch, where he and Adam kept their boat, had joined in the rowdy parties that had followed the rugby or the sailing, the celebrations of victory and the drowning of sorrow after defeat. She had cooked bacon and eggs or spaghetti at midnight for scores of young doctors and their changing girls, and between making relays of coffee listened to the involved medical discussions that always raged. Meanwhile, she had somehow completed her own training, passed her examinations, done her washing and ironing, cleaned the flat, and knitted sweaters and scarves for Richard.

Then they had married. They made love exultantly, and she grew more dreamy and placid than she would ever have believed possible. Almost immediately, Richard entered for the transatlantic race, and they went down to *Nocturne* almost every weekend. They fitted out down on the Hamble, and usually there were three or four colleagues of Richard's with them, who came down for a sail, in return for which they would help with the preparations for the crossing. They all slept on board, and more than once there was someone on a mattress between the bunks in the main cabin. Often Libby longed desperately for privacy, yearned above all to be alone with Richard. But outwardly she was serene, and Richard, ferociously busy with his work at the Central and his plans for the race, never suspected she was not entirely satisfied with events. He was looking forward with zest to his departure. Altogether he considered they were having a wonderful spring.

From the Hamble, they sailed round with

Adam to Plymouth. Libby struggled to forget the possibility that after these two weeks she must say goodbye to Richard. The weather was good, and the two men thoroughly enjoyed the sail round from the Solent. They were fit and energetic, and arrived at Plymouth tanned and in high spirits. Richard was excited about the trip, busy with last-minute details. He was affectionate but absent-minded, and that Libby might be in need of reassurance failed to occur to him.

'See you in about eight weeks in New York,' he said cheerfully, hugging her. 'Be a good girl and don't get up to any tricks while I'm away.'

As if she would. All she longed for was to go with him. Her thoughts, she knew, would never leave him.

'Cheer up, sweet,' he said, surprised. 'No occasion for tears. Fine way to send me off.'

Libby sniffed.

'Blow,' Richard said firmly. It was from him that his imitative and adoring daughter was to adopt her method of dealing with the tears of her relatives. Libby blew, and regarded him from swimming eyes. He patted her amiably, and shot a peremptory glance at Adam, who obediently took over.

Later, though, as he sailed alone round the

Lizard, Libby's soft mouth and swimming eyes returned to haunt him. He ached for her warm and loving body, and for the security she had always offered him. What idiocy, he wondered, had led him to depart on this mad venture, leaving her behind alone in London? These thoughts led him, after their return together from New York, to suggest buying a house and starting their family. A year later, Heather was born in the maternity block at the Central, her arrival greeted with riotous acclaim by every friend of Richard's who had been with them on *Nocturne*. They had an enormous and alcoholic party, and later on, at strange hours of the night and morning, each of them came tiptoeing in turn into Libby's room, bearing gifts in the form of bottles of whisky, brandy, champagne, Drambuie, Cointreau and even (several of them had this nourishing idea) egg-nog. Seldom can a baby have been launched on such a tide of hard liquor.

They had already bought the house in Camden Town, and the builders were in. As soon as Libby was up, they bought furniture, redecorated, and let two rooms at the top of the house to medical students, not only to increase their budget, but also to prevent her remaining alone with the baby when

Richard (now Resident Surgical Officer) was unable to leave the Central. Then she was pregnant again with Andrew, and two years later Gavin was born. Richard was made a consultant and was able to spend more nights in his own home. They had taken no more students, putting the two elder children and the *au pair* girl on the top floor, and making a study for Richard on the first floor.

In those busy days, Libby had often been tired, but not exhausted as she was now. Adam and Catherine were horrified, when they arrived for the promised weekend, to find her looking washed-out, ill and tense. 'We'll have another patient on our hands, if we don't look out,' Adam warned Catherine, before setting off for the Central to visit Richard. 'Have a good talk to her, and make her park the children and come to us for a holiday.' He then departed, leaving her to achieve this small feat.

Catherine sat herself down in the basement kitchen, where Libby was making a steak and kidney pudding, and prepared for action. She was a small, slight girl with soft brown eyes and dark hair, attractive in a subdued style, though a nonentity, she herself believed, next to the beautiful Libby. But Catherine had the quiet good looks that are easy to live with, and she was a wonderful partner for the rude explosive Adam. She wore quiet expensive clothes – tweeds, cashmere, suede, Liberty silks. Today she had on a blonde leather suit, with a silk shirt and tight knee boots in the same colour, and pearls that had been in her family for a hundred years, and were insured appropriately. She listened to Libby grumbling about Julie, who had been meant to make the steak and kidney pudding in the morning, but instead had taken the children for a walk in the park because it was such a lovely day.

Catherine drummed thoughtfully with her fingers on the Formica-topped table. 'Perhaps we should find you someone better than Julie,' she said slowly.

Libby was alarmed. Both Catherine and Adam had the reputation of being quick workers, and Libby envisaged a competent housekeeper descending on her within twenty-four hours to take over, terrify the children and herself into submission, and boot the unfortunate Julie back to France. 'It's all right really,' she protested, pushing her hair back with a tired and floury hand. 'In a way, you know, I'm just enjoying a good grumble. Getting it off my chest. No need to take too much notice.' She smiled her wide and loving smile, and added, 'Julie's only young. Besides, I don't honestly think I could face anyone new just now. I'd rather muddle along in the way I'm used to.'

'What you need is a holiday,' Catherine said firmly, mindful of her instructions.

Libby laughed hollowly.

'No, seriously, I mean it. Adam and I are determined you should have a break. Come to us, and lie in the garden.'

'How can I possibly?'

Catherine thought it a good sign that she had not said that she didn't want to. 'We'll work something out,' she said confidently. By the time Adam came back, she had reached the point where Libby agreed to go to Halchester with them if some way of looking after the children could be arranged.

'Only it can't be,' she added flatly.

At this point Adam came in.

'Is she coming?' he demanded.

'The children...' Libby began.

'Richard agrees,' Adam interrupted. 'I've talked to him about it. He says Julie can take the children to his father, and you can come to us.'

Libby stared at him.

He read her thoughts. 'Richard'll be all right. He'll manage without your visits for a couple of weeks.' It would in fact be a relief, he had admitted to Adam. 'She's so bloody miserable,' he explained. 'And I can't be bothered to do anything about it. I know I ought to, but I simply cannot be bothered. She'll have to look after herself for once.' Adam had sympathized. He thought Richard was entitled at present to put himself a long way ahead of anyone else, even Libby.

Catherine pounced on Libby's obvious hesitation. 'Let Julie look after them for a bit,' she said firmly. 'Do her good.'

'But the Prof's housekeeper,' Libby protested. 'It's too much to ask her.'

'Do her good, too,' Catherine said robustly. 'In any case, I should think they'd be a relief, if the Prof is anything like Adam says he is.'

Adam left the room, while Catherine and Libby were still wrangling. Ten minutes later he reappeared. 'I've spoken to the Prof,' he said. 'His housekeeper is delighted, and they're expecting you all on Monday.'

Libby stared at him with her mouth open.

Catherine's lips twitched with amusement. 'I know how you feel,' she said. 'He's apt to fix everything in an odd five minutes on the telephone, if you don't watch him. It can be a bit disconcerting. But he's dead right about this, you know.'

'You can stay at Oxford for a few days,' Adam continued inexorably, this having been what he had arranged with Professor Collingham, 'and then come to us for a fortnight.'

'But, Adam, I couldn't possibly leave the children for as long as that. I've been neglecting them dreadfully while Richard's been in hospital, and it's time I...'

'The person you've been neglecting is you. After your holiday, you can start on the children again.'

'You're far too tired now to be able to cope with them,' Catherine put in. Libby had to admit this was nothing but the truth. 'Far better let them stay in Oxford with Julie, while you come and recuperate with us, and Richard has a period of quiet reflection on his own.'

'Give him a chance to come to terms with himself,' Adam added.

Libby was struck by this remark, and the attitude it concealed. 'He's so unhappy, Adam,' she burst out.

'Of course he is,' Adam agreed, his voice matter-of-fact. 'He has reason to be. He has a problem, and only he can deal with it.'

'I ought to be able to help him,' Libby exclaimed tragically. 'But I can't.'

Adam saw at once why Richard found her a strain. She was overwhelming him now with the force of her own pain.

'He'll need your help later, when he begins to mobilize himself,' he pointed out. 'What he needs now is to look into himself, and face reality.'

'He won't do that,' Libby said hopelessly. 'He's simply angry, and he won't accept it. He's trying to turn his back on the whole thing.'

'One can't blame him for that,' Catherine said quietly, sitting on the corner of the kitchen table, her long legs with the high boots crossed, her hair flopping forward over her face. She was worried about both Libby and Richard, and the sensation was new to her. Since she had first met them she had looked up to them both. They were Adam's sophisticated and successful London friends, from his old life before he came to Halchester. Richard had the top resident post at his teaching hospital, and he would be a consultant before he was thirty-five, an achievement, Adam made clear to her, out of his own range. Libby was not only beautiful and ten years Catherine's senior, but had been competently raising a family in a house of her own long before Catherine and Adam had met. Catherine had been brought up in a servanted household, and was immensely impressed by Libby's *savoir faire* in child and household management. Then she had sailed *Nocturne* back from New York across the Atlantic with Richard. Catherine had always seen her as able to deal with any situation. To find her now on edge, going to pieces, in clear need of Catherine's advice and help – more, bossing – had been a shock. What was happening to the Collinghams?

'Of course you can't blame him,' Libby was saying. 'I don't know how he's ever going to accept it.'

They looked at one another.

'I think he'd rather have died,' Libby blurted out. At last it was said. This had been her conflict. She could not bear to lose him, yet she felt his own choice would have been death rather than permanent disability. Was he to live for her convenience, so that she would not have to face loneliness?

Adam took the statement calmly. 'I think he would,' he agreed. 'That's why he needs to sort out his feelings. He'll manage. You needn't be upset, Libby.' He gave her a quick hug, as she sat drooping at the kitchen table, and she hid her face against the rough tweed of his jacket. He patted her. 'It's a transitory reaction. He'll outgrow it. He'll find life worth living again.'

'I don't honestly see how he can,' Libby said in a small voice.

'You must trust Richard. He'll come through. He's the sort of bloke who does come through. But you must let him take his own time.'

'I can't help thinking I ought to...'

'There'll be a stage when he will depend on your help. Then you'll need all the strength and resilience you can find. It'll be important then. But at present he simply wants to be left alone. If that's what he wants, then as far as I'm concerned it's what he can have, and I've told Sandy so. It seems to me,' he went on, thinking of his discussion with Sandy, 'that none of you have enough confidence in him. You're all – you and the entire staff of the Central – fussing around like a lot of old nannies saying he mustn't be allowed to brood, he must do this and that, let's all be bright and cheerful and put a good face on it. He's not in the nursery, and he's not ready to be bright and cheerful. Why the hell shouldn't he brood? He's copped a packet, and he wants to think it all out. When he's ready he'll get cracking, you can rely on him for that. He's not going to seize the first opportunity to sink into life-long invalidism. Everyone should have more confidence in him. Including you.'

'There ought to be something I can do.'

'There is. Stay fit and well, and be ready when you're needed. Get back your own zest for life. You've lost it. Regain it.'

'Oh, *me*.'

'Yes, you. Has he to carry two people? You as well as himself?'

Libby stared at him.

'Look, Libby, Richard's one of the most stable people I know. He's handled a tough job for years. He's mature, and he's loaded with commonsense. He's still the same person. Give him credit for it. Don't stand about wringing your hands, saying he's finished, poor Richard, we must weep for him. However hard it is for us to face the fact that he's hopelessly disabled, you can be sure that he'll get around to facing it all right. He'll face it, and deal with it.'

Libby smiled radiantly at Adam, her eyes brimming with tears. 'Yes,' she said. 'Yes, you're right. That is Richard. I've almost been imagining he's broken in spirit, as well as having a broken back. Of course he isn't. I may have gone to pieces, but he hasn't. It wouldn't be like him.'

'You can measure the exact degree to which he hasn't, you know,' Adam pointed out. 'He hasn't broken in any way. He's furiously angry, and he won't play, thank you.'

'His anger has made me so unhappy.'

'It shouldn't. Very healthy sign. Rely on him. You can, you know.' Adam was sure this was true.

CHAPTER FOUR

Ambroise Paré Ward

Almost as soon as Libby had left London for Oxford, Richard relaxed. The rage left him. He lay peacefully dreaming the days away. Sister Paré attributed the change to her own importation of Nurse Marshall. Certainly she was a success. Quiet and efficient, Victoria stepped lightly about the room, beautiful and apparently fragile as a piece of Meissen, though she carried out the same duties as the previous nurse and was, as Sister Paré told Sandy, as tough as they come.

The atmosphere in the side-ward changed almost beyond recognition. Richard was calm, almost lazy, while Victoria exuded an apparently religious tranquillity. She succeeded in persuading him to carry on with the exercises prescribed by the physiotherapists who came twice daily to give him his passive movements, and who had been trying for weeks now to make him put some energy and continuous practice into the exercises to strengthen his arm and shoulder muscles. He carried them out for Victoria. Not with determination, admittedly in a bemused and vague fashion, but at least he did them.

He was hardly aware of what was going on. Suddenly the fire that had been consuming him had gone out. This was all he knew. He had ceased to long for the past or to rage at the future. He lay and was waited on by this very pretty blonde, who was a pleasure to look at, and who didn't, thank the lord, clump about shaking the room with every step she took, like that lump straight from the All-England Hockey team.

Libby was out of his mind. Adam was looking after her, he had said she was exhausted and needed a rest. Richard assumed she was doing this satisfactorily with the Trowbridges at Halchester. His father would be seeing that the children were suitably cared for. None of it mattered.

All he asked was to be able to go on lying here in this new-found peace and be looked after. Victoria's hands were gentle, her eyes pools of undemanding tenderness. He was a child again, cocooned in security, with no duties and no responsibilities.

Everyone commented on the improvement in his temper, Victoria took the credit to herself. She was elated. She had worked a miracle, they said, only half joking. Richard Collingham had come round, he was cooperative at last. They would be able to make something of him.

Her dreams had come true, as she had always hoped they might. Victoria had found her mission. The rehabilitation of Richard Collingham. Her love and devotion flowed out to embrace him with every movement. He received her ministrations passively. She accepted this. She demanded nothing from him, she assured herself. But as the days went by she could not help beginning to hope that he was responding. She knew his eyes followed her as she moved about his room. She felt them on her constantly, and when she turned towards him he made no attempt to hide it. One day he would become fully aware of her, he would talk to her, his eyes would meet hers with meaning, not as they did now, almost vacantly, but alive with humour and interest. Her belief in this future lent magic to the daily routine.

Sister Paré talked to her in the office. 'You've done well with Mr Collingham, nurse,' she said. 'He's beginning to cooperate and play a part in his own treatment. Mr Drummond is very pleased. And relieved. We're all relieved. Of course, you aren't a Central nurse, so you don't remember Mr Collingham before his accident.' She sighed. 'The change in him has made us all very sad. Very sad indeed. Mind you, Mr Trowbridge said all along not to worry, he'd come out of it.' She paused. This had brought her to the point of her interview. 'In a month or two, Mr Drummond and Mr Trowbridge are thinking of moving Mr Collingham. Now, I rely on you, nurse, to say nothing to the patient at present. Mr Drummond will make the suggestion himself at the appropriate time. But first we have to have the patient off his back and into a chair. After that we can think of moving him away from here. But Mr Drummond suggested – of course he knows you are not a Central nurse – that you might be prepared to accompany the patient when he goes down to Mr Trowbridge. This would simplify the move considerably.'

'Of course I should be glad to do anything,' Victoria began.

'One moment, Nurse,' Sister said dampingly. 'I haven't yet explained to you what is involved.'

Victoria opened her mouth to say that it didn't matter, she would go anywhere, do anything. Fortunately she shut it again without allowing these sentiments to escape. Sister would not have approved, and would be capable of cancelling the entire plan, if she suspected Nurse Marshall to be what she would undoubtedly describe as 'emotionally involved'.

'I think you may find it quite convenient,' Sister Paré went on. She was not as remote as she sometimes pretended to be, and knew a good deal more about her nurses than they suspected. 'I believe your home is near Halchester,' she now astonished Victoria by saying. How had the old devil found out?

'Yes, Sister, it is.'

'Good. I thought so. Well, Mr Trowbridge has the accident department at St Mark's in Halchester – yes, Nurse?' She broke off irritably.

Victoria bit back the statement which had almost popped out of her mouth, that she had trained at St Mark's and knew it well.

Bad enough not to have trained at the Central – no need to keep rubbing it in. They might think she was not fit to nurse Richard Collingham, one of their own surgeons, if they found out she had done her training at a small and unknown provincial hospital. So she cast her eyes down meekly and said only, 'I'm sorry, Sister. Of course, I know St Mark's quite well.' She paused, and then went on to what ought to be a safe item of information, one that was likely to please Sister, that well-known snapper-up of un-considered trifles. It was in fact a bit of gossip about Adam to which she had paid little attention at the time. 'My father's partner is Chairman of the Hospital Management Committee,' she explained, 'and I remember now that of course his daughter – Sir John Halford's daughter, Catherine Halford – married the R.S.O. at St Mark's. It must have been Mr Trowbridge. Before he took over the accident unit, of course.' So much for Jennifer Darbyshire's dreams.

'Good heavens, Nurse.' Sister Paré was fascinated. Sandy had let out the inform-ation that Adam had married down in Hal-chester. 'How interesting. Yes, I believe he used to be R.S.O. Do you know her?' she asked eagerly. 'His wife, I mean?'

'Hardly at all,' Victoria admitted. 'Sir John and my father are partners, of course, but Catherine and I didn't go to the same school.' Not likely, she thought a little bitterly. 'We don't have an awful lot, as a family, to do with the Halfords.' Toffee-nosed lot, Victoria considered. Sir John Halford was Chairman of Halford and Marshall, and Charles Marshall Managing Director, but previous generations of Marshalls had been grooms and then chauffeurs to the Halford family. Charles Marshall remembered all this, but his daughter preferred to forget it, and label the Halfords snobs.

'Well, nurse, that all seems very convenient,' Sister said conclusively, thought she could not have explained quite what she meant. 'I'll tell Mr Drummond that you're agreeable to the plan. But I don't want it mentioned outside this office. Not before Mr Drummond has spoken to Mr Collingham.'

'No, Sister.'

Sister Paré hoped the chit would keep her mouth shut. She opened her own on the first occasional she saw Sandy alone. 'I've spoken to Nurse Marshall about going down to Halchester, and that's all right. Quite an interesting fact emerged. Apparently her father's in partnership with Sir John Halford...'

'Never heard of him,' Sandy said impatiently.

'Nor had I. But I gather he'd Chairman of the St Mark's Hospital Management Committee.'

'Um-hm.'

'He's also Mr Trowbridge's father-in-law.' Sister threw her bomb neatly.

'What?' Sandy stared. She had his attention now, as she had known she would. 'The young devil. "Quite prepared to turn the hospital upside down," he told me. Never mentioned that the chairman was his father-in-law. Well, well, Sister, we live and learn, eh?' He began laughing, and left the office hilariously, only to put his head back round her door, saying, 'Get them to fix up a large full-length mirror in Collingham's room. Time we had him off his back. I've ordered new X-rays, and his father will be up on Thursday. We'll have a consultation then.' His head disappeared.

A week later, when Libby's stay at Halchester was to end, Adam and Catherine accompanied her to Camden Town. They would all visit Richard, and see how he was coming along, Adam had decided.

Libby was much fitter now. The shadows had gone from under her eyes, she had filled out, and there was colour in her creamy skin again and a powdering of freckles across the bridge of her nose. But her eyes were haunted still, and her wide mouth taut.

She and Adam went to the Central, and Libby saw Richard, while Adam sought out Sandy. 'How is he?' he inquired.

Sandy frowned. 'I wish I knew,' he said. 'He's quite cooperative now. I was pleased when he first came round. And relieved. We all were. We were delighted, in fact. The anger left him suddenly. It was like a tap being turned off. One minute rage was gushing out of him – and straight from the mains, too – the next it had ceased. But now I don't know so much. Nothing has taken its place. No initiative, no energy. He's completely withdrawn. He lies there and allows us to do whatever we think is best. You'd gather he had no further interest. It might be someone else's body. Then, in spite of his muscle spasms, he remains patient. No more swearing and cursing. He endures without complaint. I don't know.' He sighed. 'In other ways he's coming along nicely.' He went into details, ended by spilling the X-rays out over the desk. 'Good fusion, you see.' He shuffled them into order. 'This is the latest.' They scrutinized them together, then

Sandy leaned back in his chair. 'His general condition is quite good, I'm glad to say.'

He sighed again. 'It doesn't bear thinking about, though, does it? It's so much harder when it's a colleague, and one knew him in his active days. Salutary for us, though, to see someone like Richard Collingham, and know for ourselves, at first hand, how little we can do. Whatever existence we return him to is not a patch on what he knew before the injury. That takes us down a peg. Or it does me, at least. It reminds me of how little our best efforts can achieve for patients like this, and makes me think twice about going along to the ward, all cheery and full of beans, and saying, "Well, Mr Snodgrass, out you go, and they've found you this splendid job of nightwatchman, so you're back in full employment, eh? It's all up to you now, ha ha." I think of Collingham, and I know it's never going to be the same again for him, no matter what we achieve here, and then I tell myself this is true of them all. We can do very little indeed.'

'Don't take it so hard. Without your services they'd die. Most of them would choose life.'

'But not all. And what would Richard choose?'

'I don't know. Death, I shouldn't be surprised.'

They looked at one another bleakly.

'That's what worries me now,' Sandy remarked. 'In my opinion, his present inertia is a much more ominous reaction than his bad temper was. I'm bound to say I'm the only one to think so. Everyone else is very pleased. But frankly I don't like it. He's surrendered. He reminds me of an obedient child. Collingham was never like that.'

'Never. A rude, obstreperous, adventurous child, always ready to run before he could walk.'

'Exactly. And now we get this.'

'Regression.'

'I'm not a psychiatrist, thanks. They might say so. I'm just a poor bloody surgeon, and I prefer to say childish.' Sandy was irritable. 'No use for jargon.' He glared. Just so had he snapped at Adam in the old days.

'Psychiatrically speaking, though,' Adam said carefully (Sandy needn't think he could still shut him up whenever he felt like it), 'it does represent a certain stage in a psychological journey. That's why I used the word. Does he have to pass through that stage before he can take up life as a paraplegic?'

'Boloney. All patients regress, if you must

use the word, after a certain period in the wards. Line of least resistance. A form of adaptation to environment. He's merely doing the same. But he shouldn't be.'

'Why not. He's a patient now. It may be no more than that.'

'I suppose so. I can't help taking the line that because he knows it all so well he should be immune to this sort of reaction. He should see through himself. It's asking a lot, of course. Too much, I suppose.' He smiled ruefully. 'If that's all it is, I ought to be glad. No hidden significance, which is what I've been worrying about. But I'm not glad, I'm disappointed in him.'

'You were right, you know, in the first place,' Adam said. 'He would have been better off at Stoke Mandeville. Here we're all in a muddle. Not simply Richard. All of us. He's neither fish, flesh, fowl nor good red herring. We don't know how to treat him. One moment he's a patient, the next he's a consultant surgeon.'

'The sooner we move him down to you the better, if you ask me.' Sandy looked at his watch. 'Damn, no more time. Look, are you staying up tonight, did you say?'

'Yes, Catherine and I are staying in Camden Town with Libby.'

'Good. Then we can have a word tomorrow. I've got to come in during the morning. Say I see you here at about 12:15, eh? Right.' He was gone.

In Camden Town Libby unpacked her case and did some washing. She wanted to stay here, in her own home, and go into the Central to see Richard each day. But there were the children to be thought of. She could hardly leave Julie to look after them indefinitely in Oxford. Perhaps they could all come back to London. The trouble was, no one but herself was in favour of this plan. Adam and Catherine stamped on the idea at once. She would only wear herself out again, it would be too much for her, and in any case why bring the children back to stuffy London in mid-summer? Either stay with them in Oxford, they advised her reasonably, or bring them down to Halchester. Libby had only one answer. 'But Richard, all alone...'

'He's not alone,' Adam retorted. 'He's in his own hospital, surrounded by people he's known for years. This is going to be a long job, and you can't treat it as you might an appendectomy, popping in and out with flowers and get-well cards. You *cannot* visit daily and look after three children for months on end, and in Camden Town, of all places. You nearly cracked once. Let Richard get on with it. When you have him at home, he'll need a lot of attention, you'll have the three children as well, your hands will be full. You must be fit for it. That's when you could let him down, if you aren't up to it. Now isn't important. Your time will come. Stay at Oxford, and then come to Halchester when we move him down there. In the meantime, travel up and see him once a week from Oxford.'

Libby sighed. They meant well, all of them, but what they none of them understood was that without Richard she was only half-alive. Of course she had been exhausted earlier, and miserable too, because of the impact of Richard's physical collapse, coupled with his searing anger. Down at Halchester she had eaten well, slept well, had spent hours lying in a deck chair in the sun, had gone for long walks with Catherine. Now everyone exclaimed how much good the holiday had done her, how well she looked. Of course, she had to admit that to rest at last, to be free from incessant demands, had been a relief. But the meaning had gone from her days. She wanted to stay in her own home now and visit Richard daily.

Even Richard, though, did not think this a good plan. He was no longer angry, as they had told her. But he remained unapproach-able. She might as well not have been there. He told her to go to Oxford and look after the children. He sounded as though it were all the same to him if he never saw any of them again.

His indifference was as hurtful as his anger had been. In her own room that night she cried more bitterly than she had done since the first night after the Euston rail crash. Then she had been afraid that he would die. Now she wept because he had died. Died to her. She had to face it. In some strange way, when his back was broken, their love had broken. He had looked at her today from the cold eyes of a stranger.

In the morning she told Adam and Cath-erine she would go to Oxford. They were relieved, but puzzled. Adam began telling her about the details of the plan he and Sandy had to move Richard to St Mark's. Libby sighed vaguely, and said that if they thought it would be for his good, then of course they must arrange it. She was oddly noncommittal, he thought.

Her first reaction had been one of over-whelming despair. Matters were being taken out of her hands again. Without knowing it, she had harboured still some faint hope that when she had Richard at home again, all would come right between them. She was unaware of it, but she too was looking only into the past, trying to reach back to life as it had been before the accident, trying to pretend that all could be almost as it had been. This move to St Mark's represented yet another separation, another break with the old life.

No one had told her that Richard would no longer be able to live in the house at Camden Town, that they would have to sell it. Adam and Catherine had discussed the need to tell her this, and Catherine had advised against breaking this sad news so soon.

'She has enough on her hands as it is. And she loves that house. It's a comfort to her to think about it, she loves being there, you can tell that. It was their first real home, and they've done so much to it. The children were babies there, and she and Richard painted and papered with their own hands, when they first moved in. It means a lot to her,' Catherine argued.

'I daresay, but she'll have to face it some time.'

'Not now, Adam. Let her think she can keep her home a little longer.'

Adam was nonplussed. He had told Sandy

that he would explain to Libby that she would have to find a modern flat, with wide corridors and a lift. 'I told Sandy...' he began.

'Is there any hurry? It'll seem the last straw to poor Libby, I know that.'

'I can't see why. After all, bricks and mortar...'

'She doesn't think of it as bricks and mortar. It's her home.'

'But...'

'I know it may sound silly. But it's the only security she has left. I'm sure of it. I don't think men quite understand how we feel about our homes. I'm sure if you tell poor Libby she has to move, on top of everything else, she'll think her whole world is collapsing round her.'

Adam was bewildered. 'I would have thought she had more sense than that,' he said dubiously. 'In any case, I can't imagine why she hasn't seen it for herself. Surely it must be obvious that Richard can't come home in a wheelchair to that place? Steps up to the front door, the kitchen in the basement, the bathroom and lavatory up another flight. Totally unsuitable for a paraplegic. A tall narrow London house – even the stairs twist. It amazes me that Richard hasn't mentioned it, even if Libby is blind to the disadvantages.'

'From what you've said,' Catherine pointed out, 'Richard has no thought of beginning life again.'

'No. I'm afraid you're right. But we'll jerk him out of that.'

On Sunday morning he drove to the Central with this in mind. He went with Libby to see Richard, chatted for a while, and then joined Sandy in his room.

'Well?'

'You're quite right. He's simply not there in any way that matters. He's easier to get on with than he's been for months, but there's no meaning behind it. It's like trying to converse with an iceberg.'

'Yes. I've tried to get through again and again. I've tried rowing with him, I've tried being gentle, I've tried bullying. No dice. No response at all.'

'He's gone away, and hung out a notice saying so.'

Sandy frowned, and rubbed his eyes wearily. 'All the same, you were right before,' he pointed out. 'You said he'd come out of his rage in his own good time. No doubt he'll come to life again when he chooses. He'll do this his way, and not ours. But it is somewhat

111

time-consuming, quite apart from the fact that it worries me stiff. I'm afraid it's going to mean that he certainly won't be able to come to you when we'd hoped. There's a long way to go before we get him in a chair. He can't even sit up yet.'

'Then we'll have to hurry him along.'

Sandy was surprised.

'We seem to have exchanged viewpoints,' Adam admitted. 'I know I originally said leave him alone to make his own pace. But I don't like this present stage any more than you do. I think it's dangerous. In any case, he's had time enough to work it all out. I'm going to have a good go at him.'

'I doubt if you'll succeed. Good luck to you, though.'

'Thanks.'

'If you can get him sitting up it'll be an achievement. Without that, we can't mobilize him at all. The trouble is, each time we sit him up he passes out.'

'Of course, it's not unusual.'

'No. It's normal, at the start. But I felt he should have adjusted by now. However, whenever we raise him above an angle of about forty-five degrees, out he goes.'

Adam frowned. 'A nuisance. He's got to sit up and stay conscious for a start.'

'Yes. He still has to learn to balance again, to learn to manoeuvre himself from bed to chair and back again. None of this has begun yet.'

'I thought he'd be well past this stage by now.'

'Why isn't he?' Sandy demanded belligerently. 'He's simply stalling, that's why.'

'Stalling?' Adam was dubious.

'He doesn't *want* to sit up. He doesn't want to get cracking. He's not ready to face life.'

'But – but it's normal to get these faints on sitting up after three months lying flat. The mechanism is involuntary,' Adam said slowly. What did Sandy mean? He knew all this as well as anyone.

'Oh, I don't for a moment suggest that he makes himself faint. What I think is he finds it convenient. He can lie down again and not be bothered. I think he's quite happy about the situation.'

'So?'

'So he doesn't fight against it.'

'But if he did what difference would it make? It's all out of his control.'

'You're quite right. I can't prove that it makes the slightest difference. The physiologists would shoot me down and say I was unscientific. But don't you dare to tell me that when the crunch comes, it isn't the human spirit that fights back. My opinion is that if he wanted to sit up he'd be sitting up by now.'

'You ought to be wrong,' Adam said. 'But you probably aren't. In any case, the possibilities are worth exploring. Right, I'll explore them with Richard. Libby's going to Oxford this afternoon. I was thinking of bringing Catherine in with me and we were going to have tea with him together. But I'll tell her to stay out of the way. I'll come in alone and see if I can get anywhere with him. Could you give instructions we're not to be disturbed? When Richard and I fight it out, it's apt to turn into a no-holds-barred very dirty free-for-all. Not at all suitable for a nice young staff nurse.'

'Right, I'll tell them not to come in on pain of death. And the best of British luck. You're going to need it. By the way, Sister tells me – she'd do excellently in the C.I.A., you know. They wouldn't need a computer if they had her – that your wife knows little Nurse Marshall.'

'Nurse Marshall?' Adam looked blank.

'You don't know who the hell Nurse Marshall is, do you, my boy? Or whether your wife has ever heard of her. But Sister knows. Oh yes. Sister says – now let me see, yes – Nurse Marshall's father is a partner of your wife's father…'

'Halford and Marshall,' Adam agreed, light dawning.

'Aha! Sister scores again.'

'Looks like it. Who is Nurse Marshall, then?'

'The blonde bombshell who's nursing Richard. As Sister's research has so usefully discovered, she lives at Halchester. She's an agency girl anyway, and apparently she's quite willing to come down to St Mark's when we move Richard. I thought it would be a good plan. She's not a bad little nurse, and we'd get continuity of care.'

'Does Richard know about this plan of ours?'

'Not yet. You can tell him, if the opportunity arises.'

'Will do.'

'Well, I'm off. Ring me at home if you have any luck.'

'Damn it, I taught him to sail when we were both about thirteen. If I can't get the poor old boy sitting up for half an hour without passing out, I might as well hand in my chips and take up accountancy.'

After lunch Adam parked the car in the

forecourt and climbed the stairs to Paré, whistling a tune to himself and jingling the change in his pocket. His houseman at St Mark's would have recognized the signs of acute anxiety.

He let himself into Richard's room. The blonde bombshell was there, doing something at a side table. Richard lay, very peacefully, with his eyes shut. He opened them to see Adam with a flicker of unmistakable irritation.

Nurse Marshall had evidently had her orders. She went to the door and said, 'I was just going anyway.'

Richard scowled.

An auspicious beginning.

All right, Adam decided, let's have a blazing row. Anything's better than the polite stranger I met this morning. 'Why aren't you sitting up?' he demanded.

Richard had shut his eyes again. He didn't bother to open them again, simply said, 'I can't. I pass out.'

'So?'

'So I pass out,' Richard repeated with apparent torpor.

'So what, blast you?'

Richard opened his eyes. 'Spoiling for a fight,' he remarked and shut them again. 'Go somewhere else and have it. I'm not playing.'

'You're not playing. Too right you're not playing. You've given up. You've less courage than a child of six.'

There was no reaction.

Adam clenched his hands inside his pockets. Hell, this was useless. Getting no-where fast. What was he to do?

'Spineless,' he ejaculated. He hadn't meant to say this, and as soon as he had done so, he wished it unsaid.

Richard grinned. 'Correct,' he said

Action stations, Adam thought. But how?

'You're bloody well sitting up, if it kills you,' he said, and wound the bed up. Rich-ard came with it, wearing an expression of amused tolerance that infuriated Adam.

'All right,' he said. 'See for yourself if you have to. But I could have planned a more satisfactory Sunday afternoon for myself.'

Adam stopped when Richard was at forty-five degrees. They surveyed one another. For all his sang-froid, Richard emitted a very faint air of challenge, Adam was relieved to see. This was what he had been counting on. This was what he must build on.

'I can stand it this far, in any case,' he remarked, with distinct smugness.

'We'll give it a few minutes, though.'

'Oh, are you staying long?'

'Yes.'

'I was afraid so.'

Even this was preferable, Adam thought, to closed eyes and inertia.

'Meanwhile,' he said, turning the covers back, 'I'd like to try your reflexes.'

This threw Richard, as Adam had hoped it might, into a sudden rage. 'No,' he said curtly. 'Go and find yourself a laboratory animal if you want to experiment.'

Adam ignored him, took out a bunch of keys from his pocket, swung them lightly, selected one and drew it along the sole of Richard's foot. The leg did not like this attention at all and withdrew violently. Richard went scarlet, and his nails showed white where his hands gripped the iron bedhead. He would have liked to use them to knock Adam down. Adam began testing the abdominal reflexes, drawing lines thoughtfully with his key and contemplating the interesting results. His mouth was a hard line.

'I don't recollect inviting you here to play noughts and crosses on my abdomen,' Richard said coldly, sounding very like the Mincer, except that his rage had made him short of breath.

'No invitation needed,' Adam stated cheerfully.

'I suppose you think you can do exactly as you like, and there's nothing I can do about it?'

'Yes,' Adam said briefly. He looked Richard straight in the eyes. He didn't like what he was doing, but he was determined to go on doing it.

Richard was the first to drop his eyes. He sighed, remarked, 'You're right, of course,' and shut his eyes again.

Blast, Adam frowned. What now? He had nearly got through then, but not quite.

'You're going right up now,' he stated, and wound the bed up to a right angle.

Richard wore a closed expression, and said nothing.

'When you feel yourself passing out, you're going to fight it.'

Richard raised his eyebrows and asked, 'My dear boy, has no one ever explained the working of the autonomic nervous system to you?'

But in fact he didn't faint. Adam wound the bed down after five minutes.

'Five minutes. Now five minutes rest.'

'My God, do you propose to spend the afternoon winding me up and down every five minutes?'

'Yes. I do. If that rotten nurse was any good she'd have done nothing else all day long. I suppose you wouldn't let her. You won't stop me. How are we going to move you out of here until you can sit up?'

'There isn't any question of moving me out of here,' Richard responded in a bored voice, his eyes shut again.

'You're wrong there, mate. I'm going to have you out of here if I have to do it at the point of a gun.'

'Wouldn't make any difference.'

'Don't you be too sure.'

Richard opened his eyes. 'You're not labouring under this delusion, are you, that it's all psychological and I could walk if I only wanted to enough?' His mouth twisted. 'Because if so I suggest you go away and do your homework.'

'No, I'm not. You've a T.12 lesion. We all know it. But I'm disappointed at your lack of guts.'

Richard raised his eyebrows. 'Thanks,' he said bitterly.

Adam had hurt him. He intended to go on hurting him, hurting him so much that he would have to do something about it. He began to abuse him, calling him feeble, spoilt, supine…

'Exactly.'

'…what are you, a man or a eunuch?'

The colour left Richard's face. He opened his eyes for a split second, showing so much pain that Adam caught his breath. But he refused to retreat. 'So that's it, is it? That's what's destroying you?'

The figure in the bed had returned to blankness and immobility, though lines of tension suddenly appeared between nose and mouth.

'That's why you're making yourself so unhappy. Cutting yourself off in this way. You haven't had any reason to suppose…' This was hardly true, and Adam abandoned the sentence. 'You'll have to find out the hard way,' he substituted. 'Give yourself a chance.'

But Richard wasn't prepared to discuss the matter. Adam could not exactly blame him. He continued to attack. 'You can't run away from it forever, you know,' he pointed out. 'Or do you intend to lie here indefinitely?'

Richard opened his eyes. They were tired and weary. 'Pack it in, there's a good chap. No need to go on.'

Adam had lost.

As he never gave up, though, he carried on with his plan. 'Time for five minutes up,' he announced, and began winding. All at once his uncontrollable tongue, that had so often landed him in trouble, asserted itself. 'Up you go, Peter Abelard,' he remarked. They had discussed this story with enormous interest and in gruesome detail as boys. 'Might as well mobilize yourself for the monastery,' he added unforgivably.

There was a frozen second while their twenty year friendship hung in the air. Then Richard began to laugh. He went on laughing as he was raised. 'You lousy bastard,' he said.

Then he fainted.

Adam wound the bed down and took his pulse while he waited for him to come round. His spirit was desolate and he looked blindly at the six foot three of Richard Collingham extended helplessly beside him. There was nothing any of them could do for him.

He came round in about twenty seconds.

'O.K.?' Adam demanded briskly.

'Yes, thanks.'

They looked at one another experimentally. For the first time, Richard was right there in the room with him. No doubt about it.

'Damn it,' he said. 'Is nothing sacred to you?'

'Apparently not,' Adam had to admit. 'I didn't intend…'

'I know. I know.' He looked back over the

years. 'You've never known how to control your tongue.' He began laughing again. 'Maybe you've exorcized my nightmare,' he suggested, though with considerable doubt.

'Ready to go up again?'

'For the lord's sake…'

'I'm spending the afternoon winding you up and down. If we get no further than that, right. Up.' He wound busily. 'I knew there was a reason,' he said. 'There had to be one. Now I know what it is. You may be right, you may be wrong. You'll never find out if you simply lie there and let time pass. All right, perhaps you don't want to find out.'

'I don't think I do, much.'

'So you're just going on lying flat telling yourself you're finished and not lifting a finger?'

Richard smiled sarcastically and made a schoolboy joke.

When Adam left, Richard could stand fifteen minutes sitting up in bed. 'Right,' Adam said. 'I'll take a half day in the middle of the week, and get you into that chair if it finishes both of us. In the meantime make that girl of yours wind you up and down all day long.'

'All right. Now go away. I've had enough of you.'

'Don't blame you.' Adam raised a hand,

standing in the doorway. 'See you,' he said, and shut himself out.

On Wednesday he was back, leaving a tarnished image in St Mark's, where lists had been rearranged and off-duty cancelled.

'How long have you been able to sit up?' he demanded without preamble as he came into the room.

'Oh God, it's you again. I was afraid you meant what you said. Half an hour, usually. I have done an hour.'

'You're all right, then. Now you're getting yourself into that chair.' He wheeled it into position. 'Hang on to your handle and lift yourself up. I'll swing you round into position.' He began this procedure almost before the words were out of his mouth, and suddenly Richard was seated in the chair, with his legs and feet left behind on the bed. Adam moved them down.

'H'm,' Richard muttered thoughtfully.

'Five minutes rest and then back again.'

Richard was looking at the bed and measuring distances with his eye. 'You know, I think it might be better if you moved my feet down first, so that I'm sitting on the side of the bed, and then I swung over.'

'All right. We can try it all ways.'

'If I were to...' He paused, and frowned.

124

'Damn...' he began and stopped. A second later he fainted.

Adam put his thumb on the bell and kept it there. A flustered student appeared. 'Help me get him on the bed. You take his legs.' Adam had a great deal of strength in his stocky frame, and with one swing Richard was back on the bed, lying flat. 'All right, thank you, Nurse.' He dismissed her unmistakably, and sat waiting for Richard to come round, his finger on his pulse.

He recovered almost briskly. 'Pity,' he remarked, as soon as consciousness returned. He moved his head and looked round the room. 'You moved me back here, did you? How did you manage that? I've lost some weight, but I still weigh 154 pounds.'

'Rang for a nurse.'

'How long was I out, then?'

'Not long. Say ninety seconds.'

'Nuisance. Let's have another bash.'

'Wait a minute or two.'

'No. Now.'

'All right. Feet first or last?'

'Let's try first, this time. Sit me up.'

'...well pull yourself up, you lazy...'

'I prefer to reserve my energy for the move itself. Wind me up and don't argue.'

Adam wound the bed up.

125

'Now, if I try moving my legs myself first…'

Just in time, Adam moved into position and braced himself as for a rugby tackle. 'Hold on to your handle with one hand,' he said quickly. But too late. Richard fell forward, and Adam just managed to catch him and push him back into a sitting position. He was angry with himself. He had been warned, yet he had nearly let him go crashing to the floor. The trouble was, they were taking it too quickly now. On the other hand, he thought it a good plan to let Richard set the pace, if that was what he wanted to do, even if it was a furious one.

'No balance,' Richard was saying. 'Interesting. I should have remembered.'

'That's enough for a bit. Take it easy.'

'No, I can do it. Swing me the handle.' He lifted himself across to the chair.

This episode marked the opening of a new phase, known on Paré ward as the 'I can do it' phase. Richard was like a small child again, but not in the sense that had worried Sandy so. He was eager, fractious, rejected all offers of aid, and was enraged if he could not do exactly what he wanted to do exactly when it occurred to him. He spent hours practising his balance in front of the mirror, and then made Victoria throw a bean bag to him at every spare moment. He pleased the physiotherapists, but no one else. 'Lunch? Not now. I'm busy. Take it away. Bring it in half an hour.' He spent long periods down in the physiotherapy department too, and in the heated pool. On the ward, he tried to do everything himself without assistance, and wore the nursing staff out by his efforts.

Sandy rang Adam at the end of a week of this. 'I don't know what you did,' he remarked. 'But it worked. He's going great guns. There's no holding him. He's abominably bad-tempered and disagreeable again – poor little Nurse Marshall can't make out what's hit her, I don't think. She saw herself as an angel of mercy, and her patient as the martyr of the Central. Now all at once she's saddled with a bloody-minded egotist who shouts at her all day long. But he can move himself in and out of his chair unaided – Nurse Marshall never knows where she's going to find him now. Yesterday she lost him completely. He'd got himself into his chair and down to the physios without anyone spotting him (mind you, I'm pretty certain he had collaboration from the porters, but no one lets on), and we were all in a great state. He only did it to be devilish, of course.

Very pleased with himself, he was, looking down his nose like the Mincer, but with a different sort of gleam in his eye. This is all much more healthy. If he goes on at this rate, he'll be with you at the end of the month after all. The physios are very pleased with him (though I think even they're beginning to have had enough of him). They say his balance is improving almost hourly, and he's working hard on his shoulder muscles.'

'Good. I'll ring up Libby in Oxford and tell her. We'll get them both down here together. Then they can begin to pick up their lives.'

Before he rang Libby, though, he had something to break to Catherine. He went home that evening a little on edge. He wasn't at all sure how she would take his next plan.

CHAPTER FIVE

A Move To Halchester

'Sandy Drummond rang me,' Adam told Catherine. 'Richard is going great guns. He'll be down here at the end of the month after all.'

128

Catherine, who was in the kitchen preparing supper, paused with a spoon uplifted, and turned to him. 'Then it worked. You were right all along. You needn't have worried. Oh, I am glad.'

'I don't know whether it worked or not. But he's got cracking.'

'Of course it worked. Why should he choose now to get cracking, if it wasn't that you had jerked him out of his misery, or withdrawal, or whatever it was?'

'There is one thing, though, which you may be a bit dubious about.' He paused.

'What?'

'You might think it a bit much to ask.'

'For heaven's sake, what is it?'

'I want to have him out of the hospital. I want him and Libby to be together at home, instead of seeing each other only on hospital visits. I want to see his personal life starting again. It never will while he's in hospital. I want to hurry affairs forward. I was wondering if you thought we could manage him here, instead of putting him into St Mark's?'

'Oh. Oh yes, of course. We must. You're absolutely right, darling. I can see that. Why shouldn't we have him here? You'd be available, and you said he was bringing

Vicky Marshall down with him. Personally I can't visualize her as a capable nurse, but I must be quite wrong about that. She's qualified. It's simply that I look on her as that spoiled Marshall girl.'

'We could look after him all right. I've no doubts on that score. That's not what I'm worrying about.'

'What are you worrying about, then?'

'You. You don't realize what's involved. You may not be so keen when you do.'

'You mean it would be hard work?' She had seen this at once. Housekeeping for four or five adults and three children would be an unknown experience for her. Until her marriage, Catherine had done no more in this line than make her own bed and the odd cup of tea or coffee. Halford Place was well-staffed. Sir John had found no difficulty in obtaining good housekeepers to run it, for himself and his schoolgirl daughter. In her way, Catherine had been as cherished as Victoria. When she married Adam, she had been determined to run her own household, to live as she had never been able to do in her life, with her own small kitchen, cooking with her own hands, placing the meals on the table herself. She had modelled her household, not on the old-fashioned routine of Halford Place, but on Libby's brisk methods in Camden Town. She had taken Libby's advice about labour-saving methods and furnishings. Libby had told her to have a washing machine, a dishwasher, a huge refrigerator, a Formica-topped table. On her marriage she entered a new world. A new world of medicine and its demands, which fascinated her, and a new world domestically. In the past two years she had become skilled at running the house for herself and Adam. But to look after nearly ten people for months on end – this was daunting. Was she capable of it? Adam expected it of her.

This was enough. He expected it of her, and she would manage. Here again she was following the path trodden earlier by Libby. Adam had often commented on what Richard expected of Libby – Atlantic crossings and so on.

Now all Adam expected of her was the cooking of a few extra meals for a few more people. Nothing in it.

'It would mean a complete reorganization of the house,' he was saying doubtfully.

'Have Libby and the children at the same time? It would be a bit hectic, but I don't see why we shouldn't cope.'

'I wasn't thinking of having the children,'

he was surprised. 'Or not at first, anyway. One step at a time. No, what you haven't grasped is the alterations we'd have to make to the house.'

'Alterations?' She had certainly not envisaged these.

Adam had, in detail. 'He'd have to have a room on the ground floor, you see. He could sleep in the study, and use the downstairs cloakroom. We'd have to have it adapted for him. I hope the door is wide enough. And then there'd have to be ramps.'

'Ramps?'

'Ramps for the wheelchair.'

'Up the front door step, you mean? It wouldn't look very nice, of course, but I expect we could stand that.'

'I expect we could. But what I'm thinking of, duckie, is a ramp in the middle of the living room.'

'Oh,' Catherine stared at him in dismay.

'Yep. Right plonk in the middle of your lovely split-level living room, an ugly great ramp for a wheelchair. That's what comes of having two steps across the centre of the room.'

'Serve us right. We should have thought of it in the first place, of course,' Catherine said with a chuckle. 'Imagine us overlooking a simple thing like that – how naïve of us.'

The house had been especially designed and built for them on their marriage. With a view over the estuary and the harbour, Harbour's Eye had a magnificent thirty-foot living room with sliding windows opening on to a terrace. Two shallow steps led down from this part of the room to the dining room, kitchen, Adam's study, and the big entrance hall with the downstairs cloakroom. Catherine had often bragged about the interest, spaciousness and charm given to the house by this planning of the big main room. She had a trough of plants along the top of the steps, and had arranged the sparse and elegant modern furniture, in which she took such pride, with immense care for both convenience and beauty.

A ramp for a wheelchair, to lead gently up these two steps, would, as Adam knew, require to start right in the middle of the dining room. The table would have to be pushed to one side. The plant trough might have to be abolished. Adam demonstrated the arrangement in its full horror to Catherine, who stared fascinated.

She was not aware of it – she never became aware of it – but this moment marked a turning point in their marriage. At first she said nothing. A number of expressions chased themselves across her face. Adam watched, and waited.

'People come before houses,' she said finally. 'I'll ring up the carpenter in the morning.'

Adam let his breath out gently. He was extraordinarily relieved.

'You'd better make a list of what needs doing,' she added.

Soon the house was in uproar. A ramp across the living room, a downstairs cloak-room that began to look like a corner in outpatients, Adam's desk and medical journals crammed into their previously stark modern bedroom, together with an extra bookcase, the study given over to a hospital bed, a hoist, and a piece of apparatus like a gymnasium horse.

Libby was still in Oxford, where she had been staying with the children for over a month. Each week she spent two days in London, seeing Richard and sleeping over-night in the Camden Town house, while Julie looked after the children. Heather clamoured each week to go with her to London.

'I want to go home with you, and go and see Daddy in hospital too,' she maintained. 'Why can't I go too?'

'Go too,' Gavin shouted. 'Go too, go too, go too.'

Julie diverted him, while Libby promised Heather that she would 'see what Daddy says. Perhaps next time, darling.'

Driving up from Oxford to see Richard, she had on that occasion been full of hope. But in the first half-hour she knew it was going to be no good. She had lost her touch with Richard. She could do nothing with him. In the old days, if he had been in a bad mood, she had either shared it or at least known the cause, and been able to sympathize and often bring him out of it. Now she was confronted by a stranger on whom she made no impression at all. Her own confidence drained away. She had no idea how to deal with him, and she sat in his room, rigid with worry and anxiety, at a total loss.

She knew that part of the trouble was in herself. Before the accident she had been calm, self-assured. Untroubled. Now she had been separated from Richard, she had gone to pieces. Alone, she was incapable of managing herself, let alone anyone else – the children, or Richard. The emotional and physical bond between them had been abruptly snapped. Now she was only half a person. She wanted to tell him this, explain

135

why she was so useless. But how could she? How could she complain of her own dislocated life to him? Her own troubles were trivial in the extreme, minor and unimportant when placed alongside his. Even if she had ignored all this, had flung all her worries at him, for him to bear, how could she explain her unhappiness and what she thought of as her personal failure to him in a ward at the Central? He had this room ostensibly to himself, but how long were they ever alone in it? Not for so much as two minutes together. She could not imagine how to begin such a conversation there, nor, having begun it, what she would feel when Sandy or Sister Paré came in to find her sitting at Richard's side, complaining.

So once again she sat there out of touch. They chatted politely about the news in the paper – the Vietnam war was going badly for the Americans, the government had made another muddle of its dealings with the bankers, General de Gaulle had snubbed someone. Then they talked of Richard's father and the children. Libby mentioned the enormous improvement in Julie, who seemed suddenly to have grown up. As he had not the slightest understanding that she had ever been anything else but reliable and hardworking, this information passed him by. They might have been polite strangers talking in a railway carriage, she felt.

While she talked, though, Libby watched Richard. He never looked at her. He watched Victoria all the time.

At first Libby could hardly believe it. She began to watch him with fierce concentration. His eyes followed Victoria as she moved about the room.

Libby's heart gave a great lurch of fear. What was happening?

She returned home torn by a devouring jealousy, and lay awake half the night. The next morning when she went in to see him she heard the falsity in her own voice, and wondered if he heard it too. He could hardly be aware that their conversation lacked all spontaneity. Perhaps if she had it out with him it would be better? But how could she? What sort of wife would she be, if she went to visit her husband, only recently flat on a hospital bed with a broken back, sitting up now for the first time in three months, and began to make a jealous scene because she didn't like the way he looked at his nurse?

No, she must forget about it. Put it out of her mind. So Richard watched his nurse. So what? No need to build brick by brick a picture of a marriage broken, what had seemed a lifetime's partnership destroyed. Wait and see. It might blow over, or she might find she had been making a fool of herself, imagining a situation that had no reality.

But she went back to Oxford that week more miserable than ever, in a state of unresolved conflict. Madness to worry about a pretty little blonde nurse. If anything like that had been going to happen it would have happened years ago – and more than once. He had opportunities by the score, and girls fell over themselves to catch his eye. Absolute nonsense. Her panic was some trivial feminine upset. Richard would label it hysteria. It was born merely of her separation from him and of their lack of a normal life together.

But, a small voice reminded her, what he would have done in the old days had nothing to do with how he would behave now. He had been different in himself for months. He had had no need of a Victoria Marshall before. Now he did need her. He needed her because he was disabled, and because, Libby had to admit it, because his wife had failed him. She had failed to support him, failed to give him what he needed. There was a place ready waiting for Victoria Marshall, and Libby herself was responsible for this.

She spent a hideous week, and drove to London on the next occasion dreading what she would find.

Richard was busy and preoccupied. His mood was one she had often known in the past, when he was busy with some project that mattered to him. During these periods he would ignore her and the children, only appearing at home, it had often seemed, for a quick snack. He ignored her now, immersed in his physiotherapy, brisk and concentrated. He was absent half the time, leaving her alone in his room reading the paper, while he did his exercises downstairs. When he returned, in his chair, he had no attention to spare for her. She found herself excluded from all that mattered to him. But Victoria was not excluded. She, like him, was immersed in all these details, knew exactly what he was talking about, and how he progressed almost from minute to minute. Her own presence was meaningless, Libby saw. He looked to her for nothing, and it was her own fault. This was the worst blow of all. In a frantic effort to remind him of another existence outside the Central, of the family life they shared, she mentioned Heather.

'Heather keeps asking if she can come with me to see you. She's longing to – shall I bring her next time? She would love it.'

The question took him entirely by surprise. She had his attention all right. But he turned on her an expression of cold fury. He had been shocked out of his determined involvement in the training of his weakened and semi-paralysed body into the remembrance – which he had been keeping at bay by his incessant activity – of his former life, and of all he could not do. 'Certainly not,' he said brusquely. He hated Libby at that moment. She stood for all he had lost. 'This is a most unsuitable place for a child of five.' He looked at her, she thought, as if she offended him beyond bearing.

'But…'

'I said no. Ridiculous plan. Did you mention it to father?'

'Well, no, I…' She had wanted to find out what Richard thought, not her father-in-law.

'He would soon have told you.'

So that was that. Libby returned to Oxford even more cut off from Richard, and had to listen to Professor Collingham's enthusiasm about his progress. 'Physiotherapy really got going at last, eh? I knew the boy would pull himself together and make the best of things.

I always said he would. Once he gives his mind to it he'll make real progress. You'll see, my dear. He's always been athletic, of course. I used to think it a pity. It turns out to have its uses, though. Har-rmph. He'll do very well.' If Libby had not been so unhappy she would have seen for herself that until now Professor Collingham had been very worried indeed. Now he was almost gay, opened a bottle of wine that night, teased Libby, and the following day rang up Sandy and had a long talk with him. Then he announced he was going to London 'to see my younger son. Apparently there's some plan to move him. There may be something in it. Yes, indeed. I ra-ather think I may give my blessing. Yes, indeed.'

'Can I come too?' Heather demanded immediately.

Professor Collingham was startled. So was Libby. The picture of Professor Collingham and Heather descending on the Central together had its fascination. Libby dithered. She was afraid Heather was going to receive a set-down.

'No,' Professor Collingham said shortly.

'Why not?'

'I shall be too busy.'

'I can talk to Daddy while you're busy.'

Evidently Heather was more than capable of fighting her own battles. Libby decided to keep out of it.

'Daddy will be busy too.'

'Oh. Well, I could just wait.'

'Har-rmph.'

'I shouldn't be a nuisance.'

'Yes, you would.'

'Why should I be?'

'All little girls are a nuisance.'

'Har-rmph,' Heather said unanswerably. She was angry at the laughter that followed, and butted her grandfather furiously in the legs, pummelling him with her fists too, so that she had to be removed, roaring, by Julie.

Two days later Professor Collingham departed for London, treating Libby much in the same way that he had treated Heather, and telling her that there was no point in her accompanying him. 'We shall be busy.'

As a result, it was ten days before Libby saw Richard again, and by this time, with the news of his departure for Halchester stimulating him to even more strenuous exercising, he had less attention than ever to spare for her. He hurt her very much by refusing to allow her to remain in his room while he transferred from bed to wheelchair – he had been resting when she arrived – insisting that

142

he needed only Victoria for this operation.

Libby was too stunned to protest, and went dumbly out into the corridor, feeling as though she had just been divorced. He didn't want her any longer. He didn't even want Heather, of whom he had once been so fond. This was why he refused to allow Libby to bring her. He had rejected them both. He was a man in love, with attention only for the loved one. Victoria.

She came now, opening the door of Richard's room and saying, softly and charmingly, 'If you would like to come in again now, Mrs Collingham?'

Worse was to follow. Victoria disappeared, and then returned with a tray of tea. Richard of course was in his wheelchair, and she moved the bed table nearer to him, put the tray on it, between him and Libby. Libby leant forward to pour it.

'Leave it, leave it,' he said irritably. 'Victoria can pour out.'

Libby sat back as if she had been stung. Richard was looking at Victoria, and noticed nothing.

Victoria began pouring out, gracefully and charmingly, her long lashes veiling her eyes, her mouth soft and tremulous, her high cheekbones set off by the starched cap perched precariously on the piled and gleaming hair.

'Milk and sugar, Mrs Collingham?'

As far as Libby was concerned she might have been saying, 'Arsenic, Mrs Collingham?'

'Thank you,' she managed to utter. She did not, in fact, take sugar.

Victoria walked round the wheelchair and handed Libby her cup. Her light figure swished back, the wide belt exaggerating the thrust of her breasts and the sway of her hips. Libby shot a glance at Richard, and nearly dropped her cup and saucer. As usual, he was watching Victoria, and his expression was unmistakable. It was one that until this moment she would have said belonged to her alone. The look he had when he wanted to make love to her.

This was the end. Surprisingly, she was more astonished than anything else. Somehow, in spite of all her anxiety, she had not honesty believed it could come to this. She finished her tea, said goodbye to Richard in a daze, and drove back to Oxford and the children.

That night she lay in bed dry-eyed, thinking only, this can't be happening to me. Surely it was impossible that all the years of their marriage, their long companionship, should end in Richard going off with a pretty blonde nurse? It could not be true. But in the morning the twist in her stomach and the panic inside her skull told her it was.

She went through the days in a strange mood compounded of disbelief and fear, with an underlying misery.

This was the point at which Adam rang to tell her that the day for Richard's move from the Central to Halchester was fixed. 'He's coming down on Wednesday, and straight into Harbour's Eye. I've had a bed put into my study for him...' Thus casually did he refer to the conversion of the house, and Libby did not suspect at all how much had been done to prepare for Richard. '...Oh yes, and by the way, that nurse is coming with him. You know, the blonde.'

'I see.'

'Tremendously useful. Her home's here, you see. She's Charles Marshall's daughter, in fact, only I'm afraid I never recognized her. Didn't even know she was a nurse, though she actually trained at St Mark's, I'm told. Must have been when I was courting Catherine, and I was blind to the blonde in our midst.' He laughed cheerfully. Libby would have liked to throttle him. 'They live in a ghastly house the other side of the estuary,' he went on chattily. 'You must have seen it when you were here. Managing Director's Georgian – as opposed to stockbroker's Tudor, I mean. Very opulent. Catherine and I loathe it, we must have pointed it out to you. It's floodlit at night, and all that jazz. However, she's a good little nurse, Sandy says, and it's all very convenient. She has her own car, too. Loaded with money, the Marshalls, and never hesitate to splash it around, either, you see.'

Libby saw all right. She couldn't remember who Charles Marshall was, nor could she recollect the Managing Director's Georgian house, floodlit or otherwise, but the news that Victoria Marshall was loaded with money and cars filled her with a deeper depression than ever. She was so preoccupied that she said nothing. Adam had to inquire, 'Libby? Libby? Are you still there? Oh, good, I thought we might have been cut off.'

'No, I was just thinking.'

'Yes, well, when will you come down?'

'I don't quite know.'

What on earth was the matter with the girl? She was behaving very oddly. Adam had expected her to be on her way almost before the news was out of his mouth, to be ready and waiting to receive Richard when he arrived. He scratched his head, decided that he had enough on his plate without going into Libby's moods too. 'Let me know when you've worked it out,' he said amiably. 'Glad to see you at any time, you know that.' He rang off, and went up to the wards.

Libby said nothing that day to Professor Collingham though she knew he was waiting to hear when Richard was moving to Halchester. But she was locked in her own despair. Adam's news was the worst possible confirmation of everything she had dreaded. She had hardly been able to collect herself sufficiently to reply to him. When she thought over their conversation, she knew she must have appeared ungrateful. Adam was doing so much for Richard. Suddenly, with a spasm of peevishness, she thought, 'Well, that wretched Victoria can thank him. She seems to be the one to benefit, apart from Richard. She's the one in charge.'

This furious outburst – spoken aloud to the wall above her dressing table – had more effect than she had bargained for. She found herself in a new situation. It was all true and she had accepted it. Richard was not only in love with Victoria, but he had arranged deliberately to take her to Halchester with him. She was to be his private nurse. He had, Libby now feared, given public recognition to what she had been assuming would, at the worst, be only his secret feelings. What was more, he had purposely not told her what he intended to do. He had set out to deceive her. This hurt as much as anything.

Libby became angry. She hated Richard. She would have liked to pummel him with her fists, to kick and shout at him as Heather had done to Professor Collingham. How dared he do this to her? What was she supposed to be – some dreary household drudge who happened to be the mother of his children?

The rage lasted her for a couple of days. It prevented her from going to London to see Richard before he left for Halchester. If she saw him, she knew she would accuse him. She had reached a point where it would be impossible for her to do anything else. She dared not visit him, as a result. If she could not control herself, she decided, she would keep away. The prospect of erupting into the Central and making a scene like a fishwife horrified her. All right, so she would like to have a flaming row with Richard – but not publicly, not even now. She could not let him down like this in his own hospital –

giving them all something to talk about, too.

Whatever else she had lost, she would keep, she determined, some shreds of dignity.

Even as she decided this, she knew that as far as Richard was concerned, she had no dignity. When it came to it, she didn't after all want to make an angry scene. All she wanted was to throw herself into his arms, burst into tears, and be comforted and told that everything was all right. He could have dozens of dizzy blondes if he must.

What a fool she had been. How ridiculous not to have gone to the Central while he was still there. What was she to do now.

That evening, after supper, Professor Collingham asked her, reasonably enough, when she was thinking of going down to join Richard at Halchester? Would she be taking the children with her?

She had no idea how to reply. She muttered, postponing a decision, that she would have to talk to Adam and Catherine. 'Perhaps we ought to give them time to get Richard settled in and work out a routine. Then we can find out whether they could cope with the children as well.'

'Har-mph,' Professor Collingham commented unhelpfully.

Something must be wrong. What did he

want her to do?

The truth was he was tired of having his house full of grandchildren, and longed to return to his own quiet ways. Enough was enough, and he had done his bit to help. He said nothing of this yet, but a day or two later, when Libby made no move, Professor Collingham pointed out firmly that the time had come for her to take the children down to Halchester. Richard would be wanting them with him.

Libby found this unanswerable. Nothing would have induced her to blurt out that Richard wanted no one with him but his blonde nurse, that neither she herself nor the children would be welcome. She took refuge again in the need to consider Catherine. A better plan, she replied desperately, would be for her to take the children back to Camden Town. They could remain there for ever, she secretly decided. At least she could go home and hide herself away with the children. 'Of course,' her father-in-law said casually, 'you'll have to sell that house, you know.'

Libby stared.

'Surely you realized that?' he asked testily. He could see that she had not. 'I should have thought it was obvious.'

'But – but – it's our *home*. Why…?'

'My dear girl, stairs. Stairs.' He glared at her.

'St-stairs?'

'For heaven's sake, Libby, pull yourself together. You're not usually stupid. How can my son get his wheelchair about in that house?'

'Oh.' Libby found herself convicted of thoughtlessness, selfishness. She should have put Richard first. She should give up her home for somewhere suitable for him to manoeuvre a wheelchair.

For Victoria to manoeuvre a wheelchair.

She was damned if she would have that girl in her house.

'It's my home,' she said resentfully.

Professor Collingham was astonished. This was not how he expected Libby to behave. 'But, my dear, surely you understand...'

'I love it,' Libby wailed.

'But Libby – surely...' Professor Collingham was baffled. How was one supposed to deal with this?

'I can't give it up. It's my home,' Libby repeated. Suddenly she was in floods of tears. Professor Collingham could do nothing with her, she continued to weep and sob, only throwing out odd remarks on the lines of, 'It's too much to ask,' 'What next?' 'How am I supposed to go *on?*' 'I can't bear it, I simply *cannot* bear it any longer,' 'I won't give it up, I don't care, I *won't,*' and other stifled phrases which he could not catch.

Julie came back with the children from their walk. Libby continued to cry. The children stared. Professor Collingham walked out of the room.

'You'd better go to your bedroom, Mummy,' Heather said above the upset, in clear carrying tones. 'If that's how you feel.'

Libby caught her breath, gulped, and looked at her daughter with surprise and some embarrassment.

'And get into bed,' Heather continued. 'With a hot water bottle,' she added for good measure, though it was a stifling hot day.

'I don't need a hot water bottle,' Libby retorted crossly.

'Up to you,' Heather said airily, shrugging her shoulders in the way her grandfather did, which had been fascinating her for some time now.

Julie smacked her fat bottom. 'Mind your own beezness, Mademoiselle Clevaire,' she said. 'Come and take your tricycle out of the hall, you know Gampa does not like it left there.'

'All right,' Heather agreed. 'Go to bed,

Mummy,' she added over her shoulder. 'Then you'll be better soon.'

Libby took her advice.

Downstairs her father-in-law was disappointed in her. 'I should never have believed she'd behave so *irrationally*,' he complained. 'Of course they must sell the house. It stands to reason.'

'I think the trouble is more that she is missing her husband,' his housekeeper suggested.

'Missing Richard has nothing whatever to do with placing the house in the agent's hands, and I shall tell her so.'

At breakfast the next day he did exactly this.

Libby drank some coffee, and knew that this was the last straw.

'This is the last straw,' she heard herself saying. 'I can't stand any more. I simply *cannot* stand any more.' She pushed her chair back and left the room.

Professor Collingham shrugged his shoulders, followed at once by Heather. Julie left the room, and took counsel with the housekeeper. As a result the housekeeper tackled the Professor after breakfast.

'Mrs Collingham is tired and overwrought,' she announced dogmatically.

He raised his eyebrows. 'So I have noticed.'

'She has been separated from her husband for far too long, with all the responsibility for the children.'

'She has had me,' Professor Collingham pointed out, offended.

His housekeeper ignored this. 'She should go down to Halchester, and stay with him. Without the children. Julie and I can perfectly well look after them here.'

The professor frowned.

'She and her husband need to have some time together without all the hullaballoo of the children,' she urged.

The Professor was disappointed. He could do without the hullaballoo as much as his son – after all, they were his noisy offspring. But he knew his duty, and reluctantly he did it. 'Go down and see Richard,' he told Libby when she reappeared just before lunch. 'Find out how he's settling in. Stay there with him. Julie can manage here. Talk to Richard about the house, see what he thinks. You're over-tired today. Take things easily, have an early night, and drive down tomorrow.'

There could be no question of explaining the situation to him. She had to give in. And after all, she had to see Richard some time and find out where they stood. All right, let it be now.

But driving alone down to Halchester the next day, tired and heavy-eyed after another sleepless night, she took the wrong turning. The London road. She would go home. Home to the house in Camden Town. There she would be able to think out what she had to do. There, in her own home, uninterrupted, she would face her problem, work out what was to become of her and the children without Richard.

If nothing else, she could have a good night's sleep. There were the Soneryl in the medicine cabinet in Richard's study. She clung to this thought. To forget her conflict in peaceful sleep – this possibility alone drove her forward, through the suburbs, towards central London and the tall old house where, once, she and Richard had been happy together.

CHAPTER SIX

Sandy

Victoria was delighted to be out of London again and back on the coast in this beautiful summer weather – within reach of her own home, the Lawns, and with Richard Collingham to herself.

She had her car, and Richard soon learned to move from his wheelchair to the front seat, so that Victoria could drive him round the countryside. Adam noticed at once that Richard was enjoying a brisk flirtation with her. He was pleased. Richard was back in life again, responsive to a charming girl with a superb figure. Adam thought a pleasant light-hearted affair with a sophisticated beauty like Victoria was exactly what he would have prescribed to restore Richard's badly dented self-confidence. He said as much to Catherine, who was worrying about Libby.

'Heavens, this is nothing to do with her,' he said blithely.

'I only hope you're right,' Catherine said

156

doubtfully. 'Personally I don't like it. I would so much rather Libby was with him now, while he comes to life and begins to pick up the threads.'

'I don't think it would be happening with Libby,' Adam said bluntly.

'What? Why not?' Catherine was upset.

'Because Libby means responsibility and facing a new life. He's still afraid of that, and he's a bit afraid of Libby too. He needs this light-hearted interlude – that's all it is, I'm convinced.'

'As long as nothing goes wrong.'

'What should go wrong?'

'I don't know. But I don't like it. I must say, you almost make me sorry for Victoria, although I didn't expect to be. Do you mean that when he's had a lovely gay flirt, he'll drop her flat and settle down with Libby to rebuilding his life?'

'That's exactly what I think. Victoria can take care of herself, after all. None better, you'll admit.'

'Oh, poor Victoria. Now I begin to see. She's had loads of boy friends all her life, and never got married. It's the talk of the locality – has been for years. They all wonder why. Is it that no one takes her seriously, that they all have this same attitude?'

157

'I wouldn't be surprised. If so, it's her own doing. You watch her with Richard. You can see it's all on the surface, superficial, like a slick drawing room comedy.'

Catherine sighed. 'How odd men are,' she remarked. 'I don't suppose poor Victoria knows any of this.'

She thought over what he had said after Adam had gone back to St Mark's. Victoria had driven Richard over to the Lawns to show him her home. She had been telling him about it on and off since they had arrived at Harbour's Eye, and it was clear to Catherine that she couldn't wait to take him there and introduce him to its opulent delights.

Catherine spent the free time catching up with the housework. She found that Victoria had left what might be called her domain – her own room, Richard's, and the downstairs bathroom – in excellent order. She had to admit to herself that Victoria, for all she appeared so frivolous and featherheaded, was a hard and conscientious worker. She was extremely competent, and an asset around the house, silly as she might pretend to be.

Catherine paused in her thoughts, struck. Yes, pretend was right. Victoria's silliness was mainly pretence. Yet until she had had her under her own roof she had never suspected it. She looked at Victoria with renewed attention when she returned from the Lawns with Richard.

Adam, who had been working at the desk in his bedroom, and who had not seen Richard since lunch, came into the room. 'I thought I heard you come back,' he said. 'I wanted to tell you, Libby rang up while you were out. She seemed to think you'd be sure to be in, but I explained to her you'd gone over to the Lawns with Victoria. I said you'd ring her back when you came in, but she said not to bother.'

'How was she?'

'Bit subdued, I thought. I'd ring her if I were you.'

Richard wheeled himself down the ramp and into his bedroom, where the downstairs telephone was to be found. He shut the door behind him, a feat he had only recently mastered, and dialled the Oxford number. He was thinking to himself that he ought to tell Libby to come down. There was room, Catherine assured him daily. But he knew that Libby would want to bring the children, and he wasn't ready for that. He wasn't even sure that he was ready for Libby. He flinched away from the prospect.

And he knew exactly why.

Professor Collingham answered the telephone.

'How are you, my boy? Getting on all right, eh?'

'Yes, thank you, Father. Getting about quite a bit.'

Professor Collingham cross-examined him in detail about his progress, and when they had covered the ground until Richard was thoroughly irritable, he asked for Libby.

'Libby?' There was no mistaking the amazement in his father's voice. 'Isn't she with you?'

'With me?'

'Yes.'

'No. Should she be?'

'She left here after breakfast to join you.'

'She rang up this evening, when I was out, and spoke to Adam.'

'Where from?'

'Well, I suppose she didn't say. We both assumed from Oxford, but it can't have been. She said not to bother to ring back, you see. But I thought I would.' He was more irritated than anything else. She couldn't have crashed the car, or she would surely have told Adam. What was the silly girl playing at? 'I expect she decided to call in at Camden Town and fetch some stuff before coming on down here,' he said, the solution suddenly occurring to him. 'Funny she didn't tell Adam she was on her way, though. I suppose she wanted to tell me first.'

'As a matter of fact,' Professor Collingham began heavily, 'I'm not altogether happy about Libby. She's been most odd. Most odd.'

'What do you mean, odd, Father?' Richard was even more irritated.

'Crying and so on. Irrational.'

Crying? Libby? What had got into the girl?

'Never known her to behave like that before. Absolutely unreasonable. Couldn't do a thing with her.'

'But Libby isn't like that,' Richard interrupted, enraged.

'Just what I've been saying. Not like her. *Irrational.*' This continued to irk him. He was fond of Libby, and he felt she was letting him down. 'A great disappointment to me,' he said sadly.

Richard brushed this aside. 'What was she irrational about?'

'It all seemed to start because I told her you'd have to sell the house. I should have thought it would be obvious.' He sounded plaintive.

'You could have left it to me to tell her,' Richard pointed out. He had had enough of his father. 'I'll ring her in Camden Town, anyway, and find out what's going on.' He rang off irritably.

Should he ask Adam – no, better simply to ring her. Find out what was eating the girl.

The telephone rang, unanswered. He allowed it to ring for several minutes, rang off and dialled again. Still no reply. He sat and thought about it. This was very strange of Libby. Where the hell was she?

He wheeled himself over to the door, opened it and shouted for Adam.

In the living room Adam and Catherine exchanged a startled glance before Adam in his turn went down the ramp and into Richard's bedroom.

'I don't like the look of it,' Richard began. He told Adam what had happened.

'There's probably a simple explanation,' Adam said. 'But I agree it's worrying. If only we knew if she'd even been to Camden Town.'

'Quite.'

'Where's the car, for one thing?' Adam demanded.

'If it was at Camden Town, we'd know she was there, and had simply taken herself off

162

to the pictures, or something like that.'

'Yes,' Adam agreed. 'Who could you ask?'

'Hell, I don't know. The stupid, witless girl. I could wallop her. What does she think she's playing at?' Richard was angry with frustration. If he had been able to throw himself into the car and drive a hundred and fifty miles to find out what was going on in Camden Town, he would have had too much sense to embark on the trip. He would have used the telephone instead. But because he felt tied to Halchester, he could see no further than his own immobility, his own incapacity to go after Libby.

'I know,' Adam said. 'Sandy.'

'Sandy?' Richard came out of his introversion. Of course this was the answer. 'You're right,' he said briskly. 'He'll go to Camden Town and find out what's happening. He won't mind. Never does anything with his evenings anyway, except haunt the hospital or go and see patients. Poor old Sandy.' He had forgotten that Adam was not up in all the gossip current at the Central over the past few years about Elspeth's affairs.

Adam shot him a strange look. He took his meaning clearly enough. So it had happened again. Some time he must find out all about it. For the moment he put it out of his mind.

'Ring the Central,' he said. 'See if Sandy's still there, and if so, ask him to pop out to Camden Town for you.'

The switchboard at the Central said Sandy was dining at the Royal Society of Medicine. Richard caught him there, and explained what had happened.

'Of course I'll go and see. No trouble at all. Just up the road, as you know well. I expect she's gone to a film, as you say. I'll pop along there now, and ring you back.' He rang off.

Adam and Richard sat and looked at one another.

'Did you say she sounded subdued?' Richard asked.

'Well, yes, I did rather think so,' Adam admitted.

'And Father says hysterical – or at least irrational. What can be *up* with her?' He stared blankly at Adam. 'I simply cannot imagine what can have got into the girl. She's never like this.' He sounded more offended than anything else.

Meanwhile Sandy drove through Regent's Park and out to Camden Town. Immediately he was relieved to see the Ford Cortina parked sedately outside the house. He inserted his own car into the adjoining space, and went stumping up the steps. Being Sandy, he rang the bell, and then banged the knocker.

Libby watched him approach from the front window, looking down from behind the net curtain. She had been amazed to see the car draw up. Why on earth had Sandy come? He had no reason to think she was there. No one knew where she was. Admittedly the telephone had run several times, but she had let it ring. It could only be a wrong number. In any case, she was not in the mood to talk to anyone. It had once occurred to her that it might be Richard, but then she had heard Adam's voice again. 'He's out with Victoria at the moment, I'm afraid, Libby. Yes, she's taken him over to her home – she's been wanting to do that ever since they came down here.' No, it would not be Richard. Not that it would make any difference to her who it was. All she wanted was to be alone to think things out. She would not answer the door to Sandy. He would assume she was out, go away, and leave her in peace. The bell rang. Let it ring. A thunderous knocking followed it immediately. Really, Sandy was the end. What did he think he was playing at? The bell pealed again, and was followed by another onslaught on the knocker. Despite herself, she went to the door. She couldn't let that fearful noise go on indefinitely.

'*Honestly*, Sandy,' she protested, opening the door, 'I almost thought you were going to knock the house down. Must you make that ghastly row?'

'There you are, my girl,' he roared at her accusingly. 'What the hell have you been up to?' They continued to address each other, in unison, for several sentences. Not unnaturally, Sandy won, and was left at last saying into Libby's silence, '...in God's name what do you think you've been doing, Libby? Worrying Richard into fits.'

'Worrying Richard? Me? Who do you think you're kidding? Anyway, this is my home, isn't it? I can be here if I want to, can't I? Or is that forbidden?' Her voice quivered and broke, and she was in floods of tears again.

'There, there,' Sandy said encouragingly, patting her. 'Never mind, old thing. Come and sit down and tell me all about it.' He put his arm round her shoulders, walked her into the sitting room, and sat down on the couch beside her. Libby went on, and then cast herself into his arms and wept into his shirt.

'All over,' he heard among the sobs. 'No good any more ... Victoria ... gone home

166

with her … can't bear it … I can't cope any more … I'm useless … can't help him, doesn't want me … only Victoria … sell the house too…' and a renewed onslaught of tears.

Sandy held her, patted her shoulder and began to smooth her hair and talk softly to her, while he thought furiously. Certainly Richard had been rather taken with that pretty little blonde. He had not, himself, thought there was any thing in it. At the Central they had all of them firmly believed in the special quality of the Collingham marriage – he had often envied Richard himself. Envied him, not merely Libby's beauty – though it was a beauty to which Sandy was particularly responsive. He loved Libby's dark radiance, and often watched her – but the comfort and support of his happy married life. He would have said that it went much too deep for any rift over a passing attraction for a dizzy blonde. But then he had been surprised by the oddness of their relationship since Richard's accident. There was no doubt about it, Richard had not drawn strength from Libby. She had not been able to help him as Sandy had expected her to. He had come to the conclusion that this was because the strength had always been on

Richard's side. The love on Libby's. But recently Richard had needed help. Libby had apparently been unable to give it to him. Had something gone badly wrong with the Collingham marriage?

'Tell me what it is that's worrying you,' he said, when Libby began to quiet down. 'Just tell me all about it, Libby. Take your time.'

Libby began mumbling. She found it comforting in Sandy's arms, and she could not bring herself to sit up and tell him concisely what was wrong. Sandy's arms weren't Richard's, of course, but they were warm and firm, and were an approach to what she had missed. Sandy felt much the same. Libby was upset, poor dear. It couldn't be denied, though, that holding her like this was extremely pleasant. He had always had a very soft spot for her, and to be holding her, warm and pliable like this, gave him a joy he had not known for many long and empty years. He kissed her cheek experimentally. She went on mumbling, and pressed herself against him fervently. Sandy's body began to make very firm suggestions about the next move.

Suddenly he planted her on the sofa and stood over her.

'You've been worrying Richard,' he said accusingly, though the accusation was for himself rather than for her. 'I told him I'd find you and ring him back. I'll do that now. Have you had anything to eat?'

'Eat?' Libby regarded him pitiably from the sofa, her eyes huge and her mouth drooping. She had not liked being dumped in that unmistakable manner, just as she was beginning to feel cherished and secure again. 'Eat?' What had he said about Richard?

'When did you last have a meal?'

'Oh, I don't know. I had some sandwiches, but...'

'I'll tell you what's the matter with you, my girl. Low blood sugar. Any food in the kitchen?'

'Plenty of tins. Nothing fresh.'

'Go down and open a tin or two. I haven't had supper either. Soup or something, eh? In the meantime I'll ring Richard and put him out of his misery. Then we can have a nice meal together, and you can tell me all about it.'

'All right,' she said unenthusiastically.

'Or we could go out and eat, if you like,' he suggested.

'Oh no. No, I look frightful. I'll find something to eat.' She sat on the sofa still, looking at him indolently.

'Get up and go down to the kitchen and

start cooking me something,' Sandy said firmly.

Obediently Libby rose to her feet and departed. Richard had always maintained that Libby could more or less cook in her sleep. Sandy hoped he was right. The boast was about to be put to the test.

He went to the telephone and dialled. Richard answered on the first ring.

'Yes? Oh, Sandy. Any news?'

'She's here all right. Yes, I'm at Camden Town. She's gone downstairs to make me some supper. A bit wrought up, but she's quite all right. Yes. No. She'll ring you in the morning. Not to worry.' He rang off before Richard could ask any more questions. There was a great deal he had to find out before those two talked.

He went downstairs to the basement, to find two saucepans on the go. Evidently Richard was right, Libby could cook in her sleep. 'Can you eat risotto?' she asked.

'Yes, of course, but isn't that a bit complicated?' he inquired, surprised. 'And doesn't it take rather a long time?' he added hungrily.

'Not this way. This is how I make it on *Nocturne*. Simply quick rice, a packet of cheese sauce and Marvel milk. You'll see.'

'Oh.' He thought it sounded rather hor-

170

rible, but at least this was a different Libby. 'Anything I can do?'

'Is that water boiling? Yes. You could pour the rice in. Now give it a stir. That's right. Now cover it up. That's fine. There's a bottle of wine on the table – if you would open it, Sandy.'

He moved round the kitchen carrying out her instructions while he again compared his own marriage with Richard's.

Soon Libby was combining the cooked rice with the cheese sauce. She added Marmite, freeze-dried chives and sherry, and put it to keep hot in the oven. 'We need a salad,' she said thoughtfully. 'We usually have lettuce, but there isn't any. Would tomato salad do?'

'Sounds delicious.'

'We've a tin of those, and I could add some French dressing.'

The meal was soon on the table – they ate in the kitchen, at the big Formica-topped table, and drank red wine out of heavy Danish glasses. Libby had colour in her cheeks now from the stove – and from the wine – she looked attractive and had apparently ceased to feel upset. Ordered to produce a meal for a hungry male, Sandy realized, she had promptly regained her equilibrium. After the risotto, she opened a tin of raspberries, and then made coffee.

Sandy heaved a sigh of comfortable re-pletion. 'Well, my dear, this has been a much better meal than the R.S.M. would have produced,' he said, feeling he was lying in a good cause. 'I'm glad I came. Now tell me what the trouble is.'

She told him her miserable story. How she had seen Richard look at Victoria, how she had tried to ignore it, how on another occasion the look had been unmistakable, how none of this would matter if it had not been accompanied by his undoubted indifference to herself and his refusal to allow her to bring the children to see him. How, finally, he had taken Victoria down to Halchester with him and had gone rushing off to meet her parents.

'I'm afraid I was responsible for sending her down there with him,' Sandy pointed out. 'Nothing to do with Richard, that. I thought it a useful move.'

'Oh. I thought Richard had worked it,' Libby said guiltily.

'No. He may have liked it, but he didn't organize it. If anything he was a bit annoyed. This is a storm in a teacup, Libby, honesty.'

'Do you think so?' She regarded him hopefully.

'Most of it exists only in your imagination.'

'I did think that at the beginning,' she admitted. 'But then it sort of build up, and I got more and more depressed, until I felt I simply couldn't bear it another minute. Then, out of the blue, Richard's father said we'd have to sell the house, and I felt absolutely dreadful. Everything had come to an end, I thought. I still do, you know. No husband, no home, nothing. All finished. So I came back here to think it out. I decided the sensible thing to do was pull myself together and ring up Richard, and – and discuss it all. Then when I rang, he was out with that wretched girl – gone to her home, of all places. It seemed to me that he'd gone straightaway to see her parents, and this was as ominous as it could possibly be. I didn't know what to do at all. But I'm damned if I see why I should sell the house. If he wants to live with Victoria, he can do as he likes. But I'll keep our home, and the children, and manage somehow like that.'

'You're a very silly girl, Libby, and a bit selfish too,' Sandy said unexpectedly.

Libby had been looking for sympathy. Sandy had been so kind until now.

'You talk dramatically about making a life for yourself and the children. What about the life Richard has to make? Aren't you being rather egotistic? Go down to Halchester and help him, and if he has an eye for a pretty girl, then thank heaven your old man's resilient.'

'But I don't think I could bear it, if he didn't care about me any longer, and thought about her all the time.' Libby's mouth drooped, and her eyes filled with tears.

'Of course you can bear it. If it exists – and it probably doesn't except in your imagination – it'll pass soon enough. What about what he can bear, eh? Have you thought of that? No more surgery, no more sailing. Indifferent health for the remainder of his days, but life still to be lived. So you've to sell your house, that you've made so pretty. He's facing making himself a new career. Think about that, and stop acting like a spoiled child.'

Libby's lips quivered again. 'Oh, Sandy,' she said. 'Have I been awful?'

'A bit devilish,' he said with a grin. He wanted to take her into his arms again, she looked lonely and vulnerable, and her shoulders far too frail to bear the burden of Richard's disability and the children's upbringing. He longed to comfort her, to manage her life for her, to make her his own. Instead he said briskly, 'To hell with this house. It isn't where you live, it's how you live. You and Richard belong together, with your children. Take up family life again, both of you. Then you'll soon see all this rigmarole you've been feeding me with is a load of nonsense.'

'I don't know if I...'

'Stop arguing, and do as I say. Go and have a bath, and get into bed. I'll give you a quarter of an hour, and then I'll bring you a hot drink and a couple of Soneryl. In the morning you'll ring up Richard and tell him you'll be down with the children at the end of the week for sure. Then collect what you need from here, drive back to Oxford, pack up your family and your *au pair* girl, and down you go to Halchester. I shall ring Richard up myself tomorrow. I shall ask him if he's spoken to you, and I shall make sure he and Adam are expecting you and the children.'

'All right,' she said meekly.

'Now go to bed.'

He went to Richard's study, and found the medicine cabinet, as she had described it to him months earlier. Sandy's detailed memory was renowned, and he could clearly hear her voice saying, 'On top of the cupboard. That's where we keep it, because of the children, you see.' He put his hand up, and there it was, the key. He opened the cupboard. Well-stocked, as he had expected. He took two Soneryl, locked the cupboard, replaced the key. Then he frowned, hesitated, and reached for it again. No harm in being on the safe side. And Libby was in an extremely depressed state, rightly or wrongly. He slipped the key into his pocket and went off in search of hot milk.

He took her this and the sleeping tablets, and then let himself out of the house, and drove back to his lonely bedroom in Dulwich. He wondered if Richard appreciated his luck. The picture of Libby lying alone in the big double bed, her hair loose over her shoulders, her skin soft and pink from the bath, remained immovably with him. What was loyalty, he asked himself longingly? He and Libby were both lonely, both yearning for comfort and understanding. Why not turn the car round and drive back to the tall old terrace house?

At the next roundabout he went on past the turning for Dulwich, and drove back the way he had come, back to Camden Town and Libby.

CHAPTER SEVEN

The Castle By The Sea

Catherine made the suggestion in the first place.

'Why don't you drive him down to the castle?' she suggested to Victoria one afternoon. 'The tide's right. You'll be able to go along the road. I think you'd enjoy it,' she added to Richard. 'It's my family's original home – a little medieval castle overlooking the sea. You can only drive there at low water.'

'Sounds very pleasant,' Richard said politely. He didn't much care where he went.

'Yes,' Victoria chimed in excitedly. 'And I'll be able to point the Lawns out to you. It's a pity you can't see the house floodlit.'

Catherine treasured the remark to repeat to Adam.

Halford Castle had been built as a watchtower to give warning of the approach up-channel of marauders. Legend suggested, too, that it had been used as a base for piracy by the earlier and less respectable Halfords. A small solid castle on a spur of land with a view seawards to north, south and east, the approach road was covered at high water, though a bank of grass and sea pinks led to a cliff path and made a permanent walk for access at all states of the tide.

The castle at once appealed to Richard. He insisted on moving from the car into his wheelchair, wheeled himself through from the grassy forecourt into the ground floor rooms with their thick walls, and even succeeded in manoeuvring himself into the embrasure that looked southwards down channel. For the first time since his injury he was out and about, exploring something that genuinely interested him, as opposed to blankly following the activities of those who conscientiously transported him where they would. He liked the feel of the place. The old buildings jutting out into the channel had meaning for him, even almost a promise. He could not have said what meaning or what promise, but he experienced that unmistakable flicker of a beginning, of an opening into the unknown.

To Victoria, of course, it was simply Halford Castle, familiar since childhood, a landmark and a bit of a bore, if the truth were known. All she wanted was to wheel Richard to the sea wall where he could watch the Lawns stretching down to the further shores of the estuary, while she described to him how the floodlighting showed up the building and the trees, and how she had held parties there with great Japanese lanterns along the shore and a barbecue on the beach. Richard listened, amused, even touched, by her young eagerness. But when they returned to Harbour's Eye for tea, he cross-examined Catherine about the history of the castle. That evening her father came to dinner, and Richard began on him. Catherine and Adam were delighted. They could not have planned a better introduction for the two of them. Sir John spent a good two hours relating stories of his ancestors, describing different portions of the castle, how it dated, and how he and his brothers had camped there as boys. As far as he was concerned the subject was inexhaustible. He offered to accompany Richard there on the next occasion, and explain it all to him *in situ*. Richard received this proposal with enthusiasm, and a couple of days later Sir John took the afternoon off, had a splendid tea basket prepared by his housekeeper, and drove Richard to the castle himself, both of them firmly packing Victoria off for the afternoon. She showed a strong inclination to insist that they look out for her at the Lawns and wave to her, but Sir John stamped firmly on this notion. 'Nonsense, Vicky,' he said dogmatically. 'Ridiculous suggestion. We shall be far too busy to be peering about for you all afternoon. Go off and enjoy yourself. Forget about your patient for the afternoon.'

Victoria detested being called Vicky by anyone except her parents. A stupid, baby-ish name. She hated Richard to have heard it. She almost flounced out of the room and up to her bedroom to change. Catherine watched her with a worried frown, but her father and Richard, deep in their discussion again, hardly noticed.

When they reached the castle, Sir John began by pointing out landmarks, explaining how invaders had approached up-channel and how the piratical Halfords of the four-teenth century had patrolled for other purposes than the defence of the realm. 'You can see for miles from the battlements,' he said, 'and of course you look straight down into the harbour, too. It was all extremely well organized. We're a very businesslike family, with an eye to the main chance, I'm afraid. When piracy was ceasing to pay, and we'd become rather too grand to admit to it anyway, we built Halford Place and moved out of here, setting ourselves up as pillars of the establishment. I'm very fond of the old house, but I love the castle.'

Richard, wheeling himself about the forecourt, felt the wind in his hair and heard the cry of the sea birds. He longed to be able to climb the battlements, longed, too, to be there at high water, and hear the slap of the tide against the massive old walls. 'I'd like to be here at high water,' he remarked. 'It must be great.'

'It is. It might almost be a different place,' Sir John agreed. 'The atmosphere changes. At low water, like this, it's a little desolate, a relic of the past lost in the marshes. Mysterious – or it is to me. Always has been. Appealing. But at high water – then it's a centre from which you might have set off for the crusades, or fitted out an armada. You could fit out a modern expedition – it calls out for activity. It's a jumping-off point, it doesn't murmur gently any longer of old, unhappy, far-off things and battles long ago, but of today and an immediate commitment to – well, there you have me. To what? To some action far more uplifting and rewarding than any that contemporary routine offers.

All imagination, of course – the romance of the place at low water, and the drama and hope I manage to read into it at high water. But personally I find both aspects a refreshment to the soul. To descend to a more mundane level, I often come here to regain my sense of proportion after a tiresome committee.' He smiled wryly.

'That I can believe,' Richard said. If he had known Sir John longer, he might have added what he suddenly knew. Here he could regain his own will to live, come to terms with the new pattern of his days. Among these old walls, battered by the storms of centuries, standing through generations of human endurance and disappointment, failure and evil-doing, striving and hope renewed – here life went on regardless, and man with it.

Sir John read in his face all that he would not say. He was a great reader of the hearts of men from their casual remarks and what they assumed were their guarded expressions. In this way he ran his hospital, the university, and Halford and Marshall. When he chose a man for a post he chose with insight and understanding. He was in process of choosing one now. He made no comment however, simply saying comfortably, 'I don't really see why you shouldn't see the place at high water. Bring a picnic and stay out here for half the day. That's what we used to do as boys. Or you could probably get along the path in your chair. It would need care, but I don't see why you shouldn't.'

Richard didn't see why he shouldn't, either. He was in an odd mood, a compound of frustration and optimism. He wanted to be up on the battlements. He longed to be free to wander as he wished through the castle and among the rocks below it. He had no chance of achieving this. But at least it seemed worth doing, not merely a way of filling in all the time that had somehow to be filled between dawn and dusk. This was something he wanted to do. Something he was damn well going to do. What was more, he was going to get up on those battlements.

'How do you get up there?' he asked, shading his eyes with his hand, and leaning his head back.

Sir John gave him a quick glance. He read his intention. All he said was, 'Oh, there's an old stone staircase in the far tower. A death trap. I've often thought of putting in another staircase, but I never got round to it. No one interested now, except me. Both my brothers were killed in the war. We used to do all this together.'

'Where would you have put it?'

Sir John explained, adding, 'Secretly, you know, I've always fancied living here myself. If my elder brother had lived, I would have done. But then he died, I inherited the Place and the title, and I had to settle down. But I wouldn't have minded being a piratical Halford myself. To live here would be a perfectly practicable arrangement – when I'm more than usually tired of committees and paper work, I amuse myself by planning a home here. Mind you, I don't think the tradesmen would be too keen to deliver, but I've no doubt one could persuade them into the reading the tide tables and making their approach in accordance with the demands of the moon.'

'Getting away at high water, if you needed to, would be a complication.'

'Oh, you'd soon become used to that. You'd acquire the habit in no time, if you ask me, of leaving the car on the far side if you were going to need it before the next low water. Of course, that sort of life wouldn't suit a lot of people. It would suit me all right, though.'

'And me. Splendid.'

They returned to Harbour's Eye immensely pleased with life and each other. Sir John was turning over a number of possibilities for the future. He was not able, though, to go into them that evening. Sandy Drummond turned up for dinner. He had telephoned from the Central to say he was on his way. Although he had it in mind to sound Richard out about Libby, he had in fact come down to see him about a specific appointment that the Central was offering him. The post of medical superintendent of the annex.

Sandy didn't see Richard jumping at the offer. The Central were looking after their own, the plan had been made with care, and sympathy. But Richard's immediate reaction would be, Sandy knew, that he had been put out to grass, a job invented for him.

'We don't have a medical superintendent at the annex,' Richard retorted at once.

'Not previously.'

Richard flushed angrily. They had made a post for him. He said nothing. He knew he ought not to turn the offer down. He could not afford to do this, either financially or psychologically. The sooner he began work the better. He knew this but it was hard to take.

'You might as well accept it with good grace,' Sandy suggested. 'You can always do it for a year or two, and if doesn't work, find something more suitable. There's nothing to be lost by trying it out.'

Richard sighed. 'I suppose not,' he admitted.

His predicament had been discussed many times in the Central, over coffee, in committee, at innumerable lunches and dinners. No more surgery, obviously. Not a hope. Nor medicine. He would not be able to do ward rounds, or examine a patient. Pathology? Or radiology? He would have to retrain, but he would be entitled to draw his present rate of salary. Eventually, of course, he would receive heavy compensation from British Rail. At present, their lawyers were arguing the point that he had been warned to leave the train wreck, and had disregarded the warnings. But all this was a formality, the House Governor considered. In the end they would settle, and settle generously. The great need now, though, was to get Collingham back to work, for his own sake.

'The trouble is that none of these suggestions is at all up his street,' the Dean of the medical school pointed out. 'Can't we find him something that will use his outstanding capabilities? He was one of our ablest surgeons. It was not his technique alone that made him so. Can't we harness his personality and his tremendous competence and turn it to our advantage? He's a natural leader. There are few enough outstanding men available. Surely we can find him something worthwhile to do?'

'I know,' the Professor of surgery said. 'Yes, it's come to me at last. You make him into an old-style medical superintendent – surgical superintendent, if he prefers it. You know, the type who used to be the father of his hospital. There's still tremendous scope, as I see it, for an able and humane medical administrator in any hospital.'

'Now there you have something,' they had agreed. 'But could he get about enough?'

'I don't see why not. There are lifts – and telephones. So long as there's no question of a medical or surgical emergency being his direct responsibility, I should have thought he'd be sufficiently mobile.'

'It seems to me an excellent plan,' the Dean said. 'What we need in our hospitals these days are a few good medical administrators. Here we have a disabled surgeon whom we know to be a capable administrator, and who had in addition exceptional qualities of leadership. What are we waiting for? Grab him.'

'When does Havering retire?'

'In two to three years I think.'

'There you are, then. He can take over as House Governor. In the meantime, he can learn his job.'

They had put their own able minds to work, and had decided that the best method of apprenticeship would be for Richard to start in the annex. This offered a quiet and healthy life in the country. After a year, if his health had stood up to this, he could move back to London, and work with Major Havering in the House Governor's office. Conscious of a good evening's work behind them, they went home to dinner.

Sandy, seeing Richard withdrawn and uncommunicative, decided there was nothing for it but to tell him the whole story. He was afraid, though, that he would dislike the prospect of becoming House Governor quite as much as that of accepting a dull post at the annex. He was right. Richard's expression grew even gloomier.

'Think about it,' Sandy urged. 'It's an opportunity. I know you can't see it as one. But you could have considerable influence at the Central, and through your example – if you held the job down in anything like the way I feel sure you would – on the National Health Service.'

Richard looked sceptical in the extreme.

'All right, you don't believe me. My advice to you is to take it on and see. Start work, that's your need now. And start leading a normal life – where are Libby and the children? Why aren't they here? Stop being an ostrich.'

Richard opened his mouth angrily, and then shut it again.

'Yes. I'm right and you know it. You've been running away for six months now. Time you faced up to the situation.'

At this point, and probably just as well, Catherine called them in to supper, and the talk became general. But when Adam saw him off afterwards, Sandy told him about the proposed job at the annex.

'Oh, he won't like that,' Adam said quickly.

'He must face up to it, and I told him so. He ought to start work. Start family life again, too. He should have Libby down here, with the children. I told him that too. I'm afraid I've not been an altogether popular visitor.'

'How did he take the suggestion about Libby?'

'Looked generally glum.'

'Poor old idiot. He's terrified, you know, that it's all going to be a hopeless failure.'

'All what?'

189

'What do you think?'

'Oh. Oh, I see.' Sandy thanked all the gods there were that he had not made love to Libby. What would he have felt now? He had driven in circles between the Central and Camden Town the previous night, fighting a battle. He could not claim that high principle had won the day. Simply he had remembered, belatedly, that he had personally administered a sedative to Libby, and that to return to Camden Town and expect her to be feeling as he did was unrealistic. But he was still in the field. The first occasion Libby needed him, he would be there. Richard would be a bigger fool than he took him for if he let Libby slip through his fingers. If ever a man needed her, he did. But if he let her go, there would be plenty waiting to step into his shoes. Sandy would be the first of them. At the moment he was putting his energies into doing the right thing, into planning for Richard and Libby together, as a partnership. But somewhere in the recesses of his mind another decision had been taken. A decision he had never before even contemplated. He was going to divorce Elspeth at last. Bring the draining shambles of his marriage to a close. He remembered Adam, talking, of course, about

Richard, saying, 'When you have a hard knock, you need time to adjust. You know what's happening to you, but it isn't enough. You have to wait until you're ready to accept it and start again.' He had no right to criticize Richard for his slowness in adjustment, when it had taken him more than fifteen years to adjust to Elspeth's infidelity. Before he had faced it, he had, in uncontrollable bitterness and jealousy, broken Adam's career. One of many regrets.

Adam was talking about Richard. 'If that particular side of life could only work out, the rest would follow, I think. At present, the prospect of failure there is demoralizing him in every way.'

'What about this girl, Victoria?'

'Oh, that's nothing. Simply a superficial flirtation for purposes of reassurance.'

'It's upset Libby.'

'Good God, how did she find out?'

'Saw him looking at her, apparently,' Sandy said with a lop-sided grin.

'Oh, my God, *women*.'

'Yes, that's all very well. But the fact remains, the girl was right, however crazy her way of ascertaining the facts.'

'Absolutely nothing to it, I'm sure,' Adam said confidently.

He judged the situation correctly. The following afternoon, Victoria wanted to take Richard to the Lawns again, for tea. He refused, and insisted on going to Halford Castle instead.

'But there's hardly time,' Victoria protested. 'The tide's coming in. We shan't be able to stay, even if we can get there in time.'

'Take our tea with us,' Richard retorted. He was determined on the plan. Catherine was out shopping, and Victoria had to put a kettle on, snatch scones and a packet of butter and some rock cakes from the kitchen, make the tea, help Richard into the car, pack the wheel-chair into the back after him, pour off the tea into a thermos, and drive off along the road to the castle in a great rush. In the flap and panic she had no time to do her hair or her face, much less change her dress, as she liked to do in the afternoon. She was more than a little sulky. Richard, oblivious of anything exceptional in his sudden demand – Libby took this sort of occasion in her stride – was unaware of the reason for Victoria's bad mood, but he could clearly see she was annoyed. He resolved at once to be rid of her. He was tired, in any case, of being constantly accompanied. He was not a solitary individual, but he had hardly been alone for more than half an hour since his accident. In the early days, he had lain on his back thinking interminably, and they had come in to turn him over every two hours at least. Usually, even through the night, they had visited him more often. The opportunity of at last being cut off from all humankind for the duration of a tide appealed to him. He would be able to think about what Sandy had said. Was he going to accept the post?

'You drive back, before the tide comes up,' he said to Victoria. 'Go and have tea at the Lawns. Your family will be delighted to see you. Leave me the thermos and stuff, and I'll help myself.'

'Oh, but...'

'You can wave to me from the shore,' he said enticingly, as though he had been dealing with one of the children.

'But...'

'For God's sake, I'm perfectly fit to be left,' he shouted at her, suddenly infuriated. 'I'm not an invalid. It's time you woke up to the fact. I'm perfectly capable of spending an afternoon by myself without a nurse-maid.'

Victoria was very much hurt. 'Very well,' she said with dignity. 'If that's what you want.' She inserted herself into her car and drove away, wearing a distant and noticeably martyred expression.

When she reached Harbour's Eye, she went to her room and changed into a new sundress she had bought in Halchester the previous day. She had been looking forward to wearing it that afternoon, but Richard had given her no time to change. Now she admitted to herself reluctantly that she would far sooner have been out at Halford Castle with him, in her crumpled uniform, than returning alone to the Lawns in her exotic sundress with the jungle print.

She sighed, and left a note on the kitchen table for Catherine informing her that Richard was at the castle, with a thermos of tea, and that she had gone to the Lawns and would be back to collect him as soon as the tide dropped. Then, lonely, missing Richard, a little on edge, she drove off to the Lawns. Richard had been right, of course, she assured herself. They would be pleased to see her, and they would be interested in her new dress – admiring, too. But this was no longer enough.

Had she been less involved with Richard as a man, she would not have forgotten – in her pain at his casual dismissal of her – her duty as his nurse. They all feared his depression, and both Sister Paré and Sandy Drummond had warned Victoria that he should not be left alone for more than a minute or two.

Adam looked in at Harbour's Eye for a cup of tea, and found Victoria's note on the kitchen table.

He swore in the worst language he knew, stampeded up to his bedroom and took out his binoculars. His heart thudded. He saw exactly what he had feared. In the castle forecourt stood an empty wheelchair.

CHAPTER EIGHT

Port After Stormy Seas

Richard had been glad to be alone at last. Now perhaps he could think his own thoughts uninterrupted. Time went by, though, and he made no attempt to do this. He wheeled himself about the forecourt, explored the entrance to the old keep, found he could manoeuvre the chair through the entrance, and investigated further. He discovered the old staircase that climbed up inside the tower, and peered longingly as far as he could see. No chance of him going up there, damn it.

This annoyed him. He wheeled himself back to the forecourt, scraping his knuckles on the way, the result only of carelessness and irritability.

Out in the forecourt again he scanned the battlements. How could he reach them? If Adam came, and they had a rope – were his arms strong enough yet to haul him up hand over hand? What if his legs swung out? Never mind. With Adam to make the rope fast, set him on his way, and pull him up and over at the top, it could probably just be managed. A little risky, perhaps. Not enough to matter.

In any case, what did he care for the odd risk? It was not until this moment that he suddenly grasped that he was alone. Alone in a place where it would be perfectly possible for him to kill himself. They had all taken immense care never to leave him before – except when he was sufficiently immobilized to be helpless.

Now he could hurl himself off the castle wall and down fifty feet to the rocks below. That would be the end of him. No more struggling to maintain a semblance of activity, no more need to fight the constant depression, no further necessity to suffer the drag of his ruined body. No long deterioration to watch helplessly, as his kidneys failed and his circulation worsened. In his present condition, he estimated that he had about twenty years of life ahead of him. He would die some time in his fifties. Twenty years of steadily encroaching weakness and disability. Twenty years of fighting daily the battle that would never be won, could only be lost, yet had to be fought.

He could end it all. Easily. Now. No one would know for certain. They would have to assume that his death might have been the result of an accident.

They would blame poor little Victoria, of course. In fact, he blamed her himself. He knew he had driven her away by his own determination. He had deliberately put pressure on her and made her obey him. But she had neglected her duty. Had he been the surgeon in charge and not the patient, he would have torn her apart. She had behaved unprofessionally. Adam would never forgive her. But so what? What would it matter to Victoria? She would be upset, of course. She would have a good cry. Afterwards she would rush off and do something different with her life and forget him. That was Victoria.

And Libby? She wouldn't get over it. He knew this with appalling clarity. Poor Libby. But then she was poor Libby whatever happened. She would be better off if he were dead, he often thought, than if he remained – a burden for her to shoulder for twenty years. His temper was abominable these days. Clearly, it would grow worse. He'd become increasingly like his father and Paul, without their brilliant careers to compensate. His own career would be that of an administrator, pottering about through the tedious empty days, earning the salary he required to keep his wife and children.

The prospect of his career depressed him almost more than that of his disability. If he had been able to practice, he thought, he could have managed to endure his physical helplessness, the loss of most of what he had enjoyed in life. But administration. This he had always found a frustrating chore, simply a means to an end. You had to have lists and dates and times, admit and discharge patients, book the theatre, write to general practitioners. But all this was of secondary importance. What counted was the examination of the patient, the assessment of his fitness for surgery, then the surgery itself, followed by rehabilitation and a return to normal life. One of the aspects of orthopaedics that he had enjoyed most had been the hopefulness of the surgery. Often young people or children who were admitted badly crippled returned home as fully-functioning human beings. A pity no one could do the same for him.

But to spend his days in the future, not only disabled, but dealing entirely with paper work. Turning out in boring detail the minutes of each dreary committee, sending out letters of appointment, holding endless discussions with engineers, builders, superintendents of this and that about all the ridiculous details that had to run smoothly but that were in themselves trivial and petty. Was this to be the pattern of his days?

To end the necessity to face this would be like a gift from the gods. No more struggle. No more need to fight the inevitable.

Sleep after toil, port after stormy seas,
Ease after war, death after life does greatly
  please.

The easy way out. No doubt about it. Easier for everyone. Even for Libby. She would grieve. They had been very close, and she would remember that always. She would be lonely.

But his beautiful loving Libby – even with three children, some man would quickly come along and marry her, be a father to the children, companion her through life.

He found he didn't altogether care for the idea of this. In fact he was extremely jealous. His jealousy increased as he saw with devastating certainty who would companion her. Sandy. Of course. Sandy would at last separate from the incorrigible Elspeth and marry Libby. Sandy would be a good father to his children. None better. And a good husband to Libby. He had seen Sandy looking at Libby when he met her in his room. He had been jealous then. He had wanted to shout at him, 'Stop looking at my wife like that. I won't have it.' Ridiculous. He'd done nothing about it, of course, except perhaps be rather horrible to Libby.

None of this present thoughts pleased him. He began wheeling himself about the forecourt as a distraction. He peered down-channel as far as he could see, and wished he had the binoculars – what a fool not to have brought them. The tide was lapping now at the foot of the castle wall and the rocks beneath, he could hear the slap of each wave as it came up against the resistance of the massive old building. A fine noise. He wanted to see the spray flying, but from the chair he was not able to see over the parapet of the low wall that continued from the keep round the forecourt. This infuriated him. If he manoeuvred himself from the chair to the wall – then he should be able to sit there and look down at the sea swirling below. Sitting on the wall would be the next best thing to being up on the battlements. He was damned if he would be tied to this bloody chair.

But how was he to succeed in moving from the chair to the wall? He could not lift himself from one across to the other. When he moved himself into the car from his chair, there was something to hold on to, and he could swing himself across. When he moved from his bed to the chair, he had the swinging handhold, and the exercise was easy.

Perhaps if he were to put the chair into the corner of the building, between the keep and the right-angle made by the low wall, he could find a piece of jutting stone that would give him a handhold? He wheeled himself over into this corner, and found to his delight that there was an old iron ring let into the wall. If he could swing on this, he might just be able to transfer from the chair to the top of the wall. He put his weight on it experimentally, and tried out the angle of lift. It would not be easy, but he thought he could manage it, with luck. He would have to be careful not to push himself off too hard, so that he went sprawling over the wall and down to the rocks below.

Working the chair right into the corner with care, he hung onto the ring and lifted himself with the other hand from the chair. This was going all right. He was high enough now for the swing. Swing over and change his left hand from chair to parapet, and now try to twist. His body did not obey the twist instruction, and he nearly swung backwards over the wall, only saving himself by throwing his trunk forward. Now he was sitting sideways on the parapet, still hanging like grim death to the ring and trying to regain his uncertain balance, endeavouring to repeat all the compensating movements he had learned in his room at the Central and practised daily since. They were by no means instinctive yet. That was why this exercise had so nearly gone wrong.

He must get it right. He would do it again and again until he could achieve it fault-lessly. He sat in the uncomfortable sideways position, holding the ring still, while he regained his breath and worked out exactly how he was going to manage to transfer himself in the opposite direction. Then he moved. Clumsily, though. Not very good, Collingham. You must do better than that. Now back again on the parapet, and remember not to try to swing round as you did on the previous occasion.

After a dozen tries and an hour had gone by he had reached near-perfection – near-exhaustion, too. In a glorious moment of triumph he sat on the wall and sent the wheelchair spinning across the forecourt towards the entrance. Free of it. Free of it for the first time.

Then he remembered that he had sent the tea with it. Irretrievable. No tea, and about six hours to go before Victoria reappeared with the car. And he was exhausted. Oh, clever Collingham. Immobilized on a stone wall – where you've ruddy well got to balance for the next six hours too, unless you want to end up on the rocks below – with no tea and no assistance.

He grinned. He didn't mind. He'd make out. And at least he could watch the spray flying. He peered down at the rocks, watched the tide swirling and listened to the slap and gurgle of the water beating against the old wall and the rocks surrounding it, eddying back and forth, feathery spume flying out and vanishing. He felt the salt wind in his face and the hard stone under his hands, and knew he was alive again.

Then he became aware of a rhythmic pounding that he had in fact been hearing for a moment or two. Someone was coming.

Adam came roaring through the castle entrance, red-faced, his breath whistling, his expression grim.

Richard watched him, his mouth twisted like the Mincer's. 'What do you think you're up to?' he demanded coldly. 'What's all the hurry?' His eyes dared Adam to come across with the truth.

Adam's face cleared with quick relief. He had been frightened, Richard saw clearly, and now he was filled with delight to find him alive and safe. Half-touched and half-infuriated by his concern, he stared at Adam, who, breathing with difficulty, came across the courtyard and sat down beside him. 'How did you get there?' he asked.

Richard jerked his head at the ring in the wall.

'Oh, I see. Yes. Not very easy, I shouldn't have thought.'

'It comes with practice.'

'Oh, you've been practising, have you?'

'M-mm.'

'What's the chair doing over there?'

Richard grinned. 'A moment of mistaken enthusiasm. I sent it hurtling off. Then I remembered it had the tea in. You might collect it.'

'Tea?'

'Yes. Victoria brought a thermos and some scones, I think.'

'Good. Tea was what I came home for.' He went and collected it, and brought it over to the parapet. They shared it amicably. Munching a scone, Adam decided to sound Richard out. 'You frightened me,' he stated.

'So I observed.'

'Damn it, you sound more like the Mincer with every day that passes.'

'After all, he is my father, whether you like his manner or not. So I frightened you?'

'How would you like to come home and see an empty wheelchair abandoned in the middle of the forecourt?'

'If it was in the middle of the forecourt it was on the whole unlikely that I had thrown myself to my doom from it.'

'I didn't stop to work that out. In any case...'

'No need to panic.'

'Evidently. But I thought there might be.'

'Well, of course there might have been. I thought it was rather slack of darling Vicky to go off and leave me like that, I must admit. Mind you, I drove her off.'

'But she should never have gone.'

'Not Central-trained, I fear,' Richard added with a grin.

'No. In moments of crisis it does stand out.'

'This was not a moment of crisis,' Richard said coldly. 'Other than in your imagination.'

They looked at one another. 'You mind your own blasted business, and leave me to manage mine,' Richard suggested. 'Though of course it was useful you came along in time for tea.' He yawned. He was suddenly very tired. 'I'll show you,' he said, 'how I get into the chair from here. If you bring it. Then you can wheel me back along the top path. I shall have a snooze before supper, and you can stop fussing away like an old nanny about what I may or may not be up to. I like this place, you know. I shall come here often, you can start getting used to the idea.'

'All right.' It would be all right, too.

Richard began talking about a rope and climbing up to the battlements, while in Adam's mind another project began to dawn. When he returned to the hospital he inaugurated one of his telephonic sessions. He came home to supper rather pleased with himself.

Two days later – the day, in fact, before Libby and the children were to arrive – Adam could hardly contain himself. This was apparent to everyone from breakfast onwards.

At lunch time he went up to his room, and took out the binoculars.

Yes, there she was. Tom had made it in time. Fortunately he'd taken a chance and told his registrar he would not be in that afternoon. He went downstairs again, swinging the binoculars.

'Come out on the terrace, Richard. You may see something of interest.' He handed him the binoculars. 'If you care to look. Down there in the harbour. Recognize anything?'

Richard began to rake the harbour, spread out below them in the afternoon sun. There she was, moored fore and aft alongside the quay. *Nocturne.*

He flushed, and said 'I gave instructions

she was to be put up for sale.'

'Not necessary,' Adam said comfortably. 'You'll get whacking compensation from British Rail in due course. No reason to rush into economies. So this afternoon you and I are going for a sail, my boy.'

'I can't.'

'We'll see.'

Richard said nothing. He was examining *Nocturne* through the glasses. He remained unusually silent throughout lunch, and afterwards, still monosyllabic, changed into jeans and a sweater and accompanied Adam to the harbour.

Tom, the hand from the yard on the Hamble, was on board, and came to greet them.

'We have to get Mr. Collingham on board,' Adam said firmly, 'and then we want to take her out.'

'Yes, sir,' Tom agreed. 'So you said. I don't see why we shouldn't manage quite nicely.'

'You've brought the bosun's chair?' Adam asked?

'That's right, sir. Here it is.'

'Good. What I thought was, we'll swing the boom over, and the chair on it, and then we're away. If you're on board to receive him, and I stay here on the quay, we should be fine. Mind you, I think he could probably do it himself without either of us, but there's nothing like being a bit over-cautious the first time round.' He grinned at Richard, went on board, checked the topping lift, and helped Tom to adjust the bosun's chair. They swung the boom experimentally, with the chair hanging, and then Richard transferred into it on the quayside.

'I shall be drowned, of course,' he remarked casually. 'I shall fall into the harbour and be drowned.'

'You can swim,' Adam retorted unsympathetically. 'And the flood's on.' He knew Richard was in fact unworried. He was assessing distances with his eye. Nothing would have stopped him making the attempt.

'Right,' he said suddenly. 'Let her go, then.'

'Here you go.' Adam pushed gently on the boom. Tom hauled in, and Richard swung out from the quayside over the cockpit of *Nocturne*, where Tom held on to him. Adam hopped on board, and between them they had Richard on the steering seat. He held on to the tiller with one hand and the cockpit coaming with the other, his face taut, concentrated, his balance uncertain. Adam stowed the bosun's chair below, then conferred with Tom, checked ropes and fenders, and put out his own charts that he had brought with him for this trip. Then he disappeared into the cabin again, rummaged in the lockers, and came out with a harness.

'You wear this,' he said flatly.

Richard scowled. 'That's for the open Atlantic in Force Eight. Not for mooring in the Hal in Force Three or Four.'

'It's for you, now.'

Their eyes locked.

'Have some sense,' Adam suggested. 'You haven't even tried to balance when she's under way. Use your head. Wear the harness.'

There was silence.

'All right.' Richard gave in suddenly. 'I suppose so.' He ducked his head and Adam fixed the harness for him. Richard started the engine, Adam went to the stern rope. Tom was in the bow.

'Ready to cast off.'

'Right. Ready to cast off forward?'

'Ready, sir.'

'Right. Cast off forward.' The bow swung out into the stream as Richard put the engine slowly ahead. 'Cast off aft.' They moved gently out into the river, Richard remaining at the helm. He grinned at Adam. 'Not exactly single-handed,' he remarked. 'But a good deal better than I'd expected.'

'I'll show you the charts. What I thought we might do…' He explained the sail he thought they might have, and guided Richard downstream. 'There's the Lawns,' he added, his eyes crinkling with amusement. 'Pity it's not dark, and you could see the floodlighting, eh?' They both laughed. In ten minutes they were out of the estuary and at sea. Adam and Tom hoisted the mainsail, and then the jib, and they were sailing, heeled over nicely in a Force Four breeze from the north. They sailed for a couple of hours with Richard at the helm and the other two as crew, ending with a hard tack back into the harbour. Richard had been taciturn throughout – he had after all had a double job on his hands, sailing the boat and maintaining his own balance as they went about on each tack – but there was a light in his eyes that had been missing since the rail disaster.

Then they made fast, extricated Richard from the cockpit into his wheelchair, and tried to settle up with Tom. He, however, refused to accept any cash at all, saying definitely, 'It has been a privilege to come with you, sir, on your first sail since your accident. I'm grateful to you for asking me.'

'Didn't ask you. You and that interfering

devil over there fixed it up between you, behind my back.'

'We've had a good sail, anyway, sir. And I'm glad to see you so fit, and I'm not taking no money off you, thank you all the same, sir.' They compromised by all going into the Dolphin for a drink together, before Tom returned to the Hamble. Then Adam drove back to the Harbour's Eye, where supper was overdue.

Richard and Adam were lethargic with sun and wind, and voraciously hungry. They decided not to change for the meal, and sat down in sweaters and jeans, their hair tousled and their skin salty. Richard was more relaxed than Adam had seen him for months. He had a temptation to open a celebration bottle of wine, but decided this would be to make too much of the achievement, and fetched beer instead. They drank deeply, and ate heartily of the liver, bacon, sausages and tomatoes provided by Catherine. They said little – too busy stuffing themselves, Catherine thought with rueful amusement, while she listened to Victoria expatiating on some simply gorgeous material she has seen in Blundell's in Halchester that afternoon, and how she thought it would make up into truly luscious beachwear.

'We saw the Lawns, of course, as we went downstream,' Adam came out of his abstraction to remark, a malicious gleam in his eye.

Victoria, unnoticing, responded as he had intended. 'Oh,' she exclaimed at once, '*what* a pity you couldn't have seen it floodlit.'

Adam remained poker-faced. Richard shot him a glance, and his own expression became one of studied blankness. Catherine's lips curved, but she said only, 'Tell me about those Japanese lanterns, Vicky, that you bought in London – where did you say you found them?' She thought she owed the poor girl this inquiry, as the men were being so devilish to her.

Victoria launched herself happily into an account of a shopping expedition to Knightsbridge and Sloane Square, followed by a detailed account of a party at the Lawns, who had come, what she had worn, and what they had all eaten. Catherine listened patiently and asked the right questions, while Richard and Adam began discussing *Nocturne*'s sailing ability against the wind.

That night Richard went to bed cheerful and slept like a log.

Adam and Catherine, upstairs in their own bedroom, discussed the sail. 'He was all right, you know,' Adam said with relief. 'It was a bit of an outside chance, but it came off, thank God. He can handle that boat perfectly still. That should buck him up. His sailing days are by no means over. If that job down here comes to anything, I think it would suit him much better than being in London. Let's face it, no job is going to mean as much to him as surgery, but if he can spend his free time sailing…'

'He looked quite different this evening, I thought. More like he used to be. Just that one sail made a tremendous difference to his outlook, no doubt about it.'

'Another thing that should make a difference, too, and from tomorrow, is that darling Victoria will be sleeping at the floodlit Lawns, instead of here. That will please him. He's been feeling too cosseted. He's in a very independent frame of mind, and good luck to him.'

'Tomorrow Libby and the children arrive,' Catherine pointed out. 'It's the garden party as well,' she added. 'So everyone can have their minds taken off their troubles by joining in the annual revels of Halford and Marshall, all wearing their most super clothes. No doubt Victoria will have an outfit to stun us all.'

She was right. The next day Victoria came

drifting into her room to display herself in floating green voile. Green feathers framed her slim neck in the latest fashion, and bordered the wide almost medieval sleeves, fluttering as she moved her hands. Her gleaming blonde hair shone under a drooping green organdie hat that might have dated from the thirties, she carried a matching green bag and wore ribbon sandals of the identical colour. She was utterly charming, totally feminine. Catherine could not help admiring the picture she made and yet at the same time was a little sad. All this for the works' party? Then she blamed herself for her slowness. All this for Richard Collingham, of course. A last throw, presumably, before Libby's reappearance on the scene. Catherine felt sad again. Victoria hadn't a hope, she knew. At the same time, though, she wondered how Libby would take Victoria's brilliant appearance, when she herself arrived tired after a long drive with three fractious children. Suddenly inspired, Catherine said 'It's gorgeous, Vicky. I love it. You'll stun them all. Look, why don't you go on ahead, as you're ready? I shall be held up because of waiting for Libby. You go on and support Dad. You certainly look the part. *One* of us ought to be around from the beginning.'

Victoria had accepted the suggestion with gratitude, and shortly afterwards Catherine heard her drive off. She congratulated herself on a piece of tactful good management – but too soon. Richard had gone also. He was nowhere to be seen, and there was no sign of his wheelchair. She hardly had time to take this in, when Libby drove up.

Catherine coped as well as she could, putting forward on the spur of the moment what she regarded as a distinctly unlikely story that Richard had gone early to Halford House to help her father, as Adam was held up at St. Mark's. Libby appeared to accept this, and she and Julie took the children upstairs to wash and change.

Catherine immediately shut herself into Richard's room downstairs and telephoned Adam. She told him what had happened. 'No need to panic,' he said equably. 'I'll ring your father. He can detach Richard from darling Victoria, and by the time Libby arrives all will be under control.'

'You do think that's where they both are, don't you? I mean, they haven't cleared off somewhere?'

'Nonsense,' Adam said confidently. 'Richard wouldn't be so daft. He probably funked

216

meeting the children for the first time in a wheelchair. I don't suppose it's any more than that. Not to worry.' He rang off in his usual abrupt way, dialled Halford Place, bullied the housekeeper into searching for Sir John in the grounds and bringing him to the telephone.

'Oh, yes, they're here,' Sir John said. 'You can't miss 'em. Vicky done up like something out of *Vogue*, and with the sort of hat my mother used to wear to these affairs. Extraordinary. They're what that generation might have called the cynosure of all eyes. Vicky and her floppy hat drooping gallantly over our hero in his chair.'

'Separate them.'

'If you like, my boy.' Sir John was undisturbed.

'Libby and Catherine will be with you in half an hour or so. It would be a pity if Libby's first sight of Richard was with darling Vicky wrapping herself around him.'

'Point taken. One of my young men can take on mademoiselle, and I want to have a talk to Richard myself about that job.'

Meanwhile at Harbour's Eye, Catherine brought the car round.

'It's going to be a bit of a squash, I'm afraid,' she apologised when Libby appeared with Julie and the three children. 'But we can manage. If Julie goes in the back with Heather and Andrew, and you have Gavin on your lap.'

'That's perfect,' Libby said serenely. She was in dead panic, but none of it showed. She might have been any self-possessed young mother taking her children out for the afternoon, dressed in their best. She was looking her most poised, tall, long-legged, her dark hair shining, drawn into a great chignon low on her neck, her skin clear and lightly freckled by the sun, her wide mouth gentle. Her sleeveless dress of heavy beige silk, with the latest high collar, emphasized her slender beauty and her quiet elegance. The children, momentarily clean and tidy, wore blue gingham – Heather a brief dress with short sleeves displaying her fat arms, and the two boys in gingham shirts and plain blue shorts. Three dark heads were brushed neatly. All of them looked far too good to be true.

'Did you say there'd be strawberries?' Andrew demanded for the tenth time.

'Daddy will be there,' Heather said reproachfully, drawing down her long upper lip like her grandfather.

'I know. But will there be stwawbwies?'

'You shouldn't be thinking about *food*,'

218

Heather said disgustedly, 'when Daddy...'

'I expect there are certain to be straw-berries,' Catherine said pacifically. 'There usually are. And ice cream too.'

'Stwawbwies and nicecweam?'

'Ice cream, darling,' Libby said auto-matically.

'I know. That's what I said. Stwawbwies and nicecweam.'

'Nicecweam,' Gavin announced, taking his thumb out of his mouth. 'Nicecweam. Nicecweam.' He laughed happily, and bounced up and down on Libby's knee, shouting, 'Nicecweam, nicecweam,' until Andrew joined him, and they tried to out-shriek one another. In the din nothing else could be heard, and the adults subsided into silence. Libby asked herself once again why Richard had not been at Harbour's Eye to meet her, and where Victoria was? Nothing would have induced her to ask Catherine about either of those two points. She felt the confidence draining out of her with every bounce Gavin made. *Where was Richard?*

Catherine turned in at the drive and drove up to the Palladian portico of Halford Place. 'We'll go and find my father,' she said, and led the way through the spacious empty hall, through the formal drawing room with the

French furniture and the chandelier – always opened up for the garden party – and out on to the terrace overlooking the gardens.

On this perfect summer afternoon, the gardens were at their best – though crowded, with pretty dresses, a marquee, clusters of little tables here and there under the trees, clock golf on one lawn, croquet on another, a flower show, a baby show, children tearing about everywhere, and a programme of races being organized by a team from Halford and Marshall.

'Stwawbwies, stwawbwies and nicecweam.' Andrew had unerringly spotted the occupation of those who were seated at the little tables.

'Yes, darling, in a minute.'

'Nicecweam, nicecweam,' Gavin took up the cry.

'All right, darling, soon.'

'I take them, Libby,' Julie suggested. 'I take them for strawberries, yes, and you find Reechard. No?'

'Yes,' Catherine said at once. 'What a good idea.'

'I don't want any old strawberries,' Heather announced scornfully. 'I want Daddy.'

'You come with me, then, darling and let the boys go with Julie,' Libby agreed.

'There should be some champagne somewhere about,' Catherine said, peering here
and there. Champagne was traditional at
the garden party. A waiter emerged from the
crowd, gave her a cheerful grin, (he was one
of the estate workmen, pressed into service
for the occasion) and said, 'There's a special
tray for you in the drawing room, we were to
tell you, Mrs. Trowbridge, and Sir John is
expecting you down by the rose garden.'

'Oh, thank you, Alec. How marvellous.
Come on, Libby, let's grab, and then we'll
go down and find Dad.' She turned back
towards the drawing room windows.

'Shall I come and open it for you?' Alec
asked her. He was an old friend, who in
boyhood had shown her birds' nests and
where the cygnets were to be found, and who
in later years told her all about his children,
and the mileage he could get out of his car.

'Yes, Alec, do please. It always goes pop
when I do it, and shoots all over me.'

'It does that for me too,' Alec agreed. 'I
drenched the vicar earlier on. But I'm getting the hang of it now.' He began fiddling
with the wire. Heather attached herself to
him and watched fascinated. 'Why does it
pop out like that when you take that wire
off?' she asked.

'Well, you see, it's gassy, like, and…'

'Gassy?'

'Like fizzy lemonade,' Alec explained. 'And there's some of that here for you too, I see. I'll pour it out for you in a minute.'

'Can't I have some of the other stuff?'

'You must ask your mother,' Alec said cautiously.

'Mummy, Mummy, can I have some of that stuff you're drinking?'

'You can taste mine, if you like. It'll probably go up your nose.' She handed her glass to Heather. 'Be careful, don't spill it.'

Heather wrinkled her nose. 'I don't think much of *that*. And it does go up your nose. I think it's a rather silly drink.'

'Good.'

'So can I have some fizzy lemonade then?'

Alec handed her some, in a champagne glass, and she drank with obvious gusto. 'Much nicer,' she pronounced.

Libby and Catherine exchanged glances. 'Just as well, I must say,' Libby remarked.

'Why just as well?'

'Because champagne is very expensive, and I couldn't afford to buy it for you if you did like it.'

'Oh. Well then, why…'

'Now we'll go and look for Daddy,' Libby

said hastily, before Heather could insist on having a breakdown of the details of the Halford budget for the garden party. They made their way down to the rose garden, where there was a group of chairs by the sundial. Libby tried to find Richard there, but she had not succeeded in spotting him when there was a sudden shriek from her side and Heather had gone. 'Daddy, Daddy,' she yelled, and launched herself into the crowd.

For Richard, this was the moment when he knew without a doubt that one at least of his fears was groundless. Heather appeared not to notice that he was in a wheelchair. He was Daddy, and she had found him. That was all there was to it. She sat on his knee, and explained to him that she didn't think much of champagne.

'Oh, don't you?' he said. Libby had joined them, and he caught her eye, without even knowing he had done so. 'I daresay that's just as well.'

'That's what Mummy said.'

'I agree with her.'

'Har-rmph.'

Richard was disconcerted. He had not heard Heather produce this reproduction of his father's famous set-down before, and his eyes flew again, automatically, to Libby. She met his glance with eyes brimming with suppressed mirth. Suddenly it was as if they had never been apart. Both of them wondered, fleetingly, what their agonizing had been about. Here they were. They belonged together.

Julie appeared with the other two children. 'They've been having stwawbwies,' Heather said scathingly. 'I came to see you first.'

'I thought you were having champagne.'

'Oh, *that*.'

'Get down now, I want to talk to Andrew.'

'Stwawbwies and nicecweam, I had,' Andrew stated. 'Up,' he added peremptorily. 'Up.'

Richard lifted him onto his knee.

'Stwawbwies and nicecweam.'

'Yes, I've got that,' Richard agreed.

Gavin began jumping up and down and crying.

'I'm afraid he's feeling left out,' Libby said.

'He's only a baby,' Heather explained.

'When you were only a baby,' Richard said firmly, finding his daughter in need of a set-down herself, 'we used to cart you about in a carry-cot, and...'

'Me? In one of *those* things?'

'Yes. You. In one of those things. While we

painted the house – do you remember, Lib?'

Did she remember? She could never forget those days in the Camden Town house. Would they ever have another home that meant as much to them?

'Gampa says we'll have to sell the house,' Heather pointed out bossily.

'Heather…'

'Gampa is right,' Richard said firmly. 'He usually is, you know. We have to look for another one.'

'Why?'

'Because I can't go up and down stairs in this thing.' He patted the wheelchair.

Heather appeared to see it for the first time. 'Why can't you get out of it and walk up?' she asked.

'Because my legs don't work any more.'

'Oh.' She digested this. 'Can't they do something about it – at the Central?'

'No. They've tried, but they can't.'

'Oh. I should have thought they could,' she said with some disapproval. She looked thoughtfully at him, and prodded his knee experimentally. Richard had a distinct impression that she might possibly arrange some method to restore him to full mobility.

Gavin, who had paused temporarily while the conversation went on round him, took a deep breath and renewed his outcry.

'Get down, Andrew, and let Gavin come up here,' Richard said hastily. He reached down and scooped up his youngest, who put his thumb in his mouth and settled comfortably back with a beatific expression.

Julie and Catherine persuaded the other two children in the direction of the marquee, and Libby and Richard were left. He put his hand out to her, saying 'Come here. All these kids climbing all over me, and I can't get near you.' Libby pressed her cheek against his, and wondered why she had ever imagined it mattered about the house. Richard apparently read her thoughts and asked, 'Do you mind very much about the house?'

'No, of course not,' she said indignantly and untruthfully.

'I thought you would. I was waiting to tell you. Why on earth father had to butt in – though I supposed I might have known. In any case – I've been offered a job. Or rather, two jobs.' He paused.

'Two jobs? What?'

'One of them is to be medical super-intendent at the annex for a year or two, with the idea of going to the House Governor's office, after that, and then taking over when Havering retires.' He frowned, and

Libby didn't need to ask what he thought of that plan.

'And the other?'

'Ah yes. The other.' The other possibility had been put before him only in the past hour. 'The other is more of a toss-up,' he said slowly. Gavin took his thumb out of his mouth, enunciated with clarity, 'Toss-up,' and put it back in again. 'That's right,' Richard agreed. 'It's a toss-up, old boy.' He stared into the distance. 'I don't know. It has possibilities.'

Sir John Halford had offered him the post of Director of the Student Health Service at the new university of Halchester.

'It would have to be built up from the beginning,' he had explained. 'Nothing has been laid down. You would begin in a small way – like the university itself. But in five years' time the university will have two thousand places, and be a going concern.'

What attracted Richard was this opportunity to build the service from nothing. He would enjoy that.

'I'm afraid we're still a figment of the imagination, here,' Sir John admitted, 'though we do expect two hundred undergraduates next month, who are being lodged round the town until the halls of residence are ready. But for the next ten years we're going to be no more than one of those bleak new universities somewhere down on the coast. Nothing comparable to a centuries-old teaching hospital with traditions like the Central – and I'm told you would be House Governor there within five years.'

'Hmph,' Richard said unmistakably.

'You can't afford to look askance at that. On the other hand, I had a notion that you might possibly prefer to be in at the beginning of a new departure. I thought, too (and Adam agreed with me) that you might find living down here more to your liking than central London.'

'You're right there.' The plan came as a tremendous relief. That was the only way to put it. Here was no perfect job, of course. But the post was genuine. Someone had to hold the job down and establish the service. Why not him? He took a deep breath of thankfulness. Here was no sinecure.

'If you want it,' Sir John had said, 'the job's yours. You'd have to be formally approved by the Committee, of course, but there'd be no difficulty about that. The appointment, I should have said, is not actually made by the university. This would be a service run on behalf of the university at first, (at any rate) by St Mark's, and the appointment will be made by the St Mark's Hospital Management Committee.'

All became clear. Richard grinned. All he had to do was to say yes.

'How do you feel about it?' Sir John asked.

'I like the idea very much,' Richard said slowly. 'It appeals to me far more than the administrative post the Central has found me. My only doubt is whether I can do it.'

Sir John came briskly down to earth. 'On the whole,' he pointed out, 'the students would come to you, rather than you go to them. There would be a certain number of visits to be made, naturally, from time to time, but I think the idea is that you could perhaps have the G.P.s on a rotation for that sort of activity. It would need careful planning but that would be up to you.'

'It seems to me,' Richard said accurately, 'that Adam has had a go at working it out.'

Sir John drummed with his fingers on the little round table. 'I mentioned it to my son-in-law,' he admitted. 'Of course.'

'I'm very grateful to you both,' Richard said. To his surprise this remark, which he had embarked on in duty, since he owed it to Adam to be at least polite to his father-in-law, when the old boy had clearly gone to a good deal of trouble, came out with genuine warmth. He was grateful, and he wanted to take the job. Of course it didn't come anywhere near being a surgeon on the staff at the Central, but it was a great deal more tolerable as a way of life than being chief administrator there.

'You think it over for a day or two, and let me know,' Sir John suggested. He rubbed his nose, looked mysterious and, Richard was almost certain, a little excited. He was planning to make the castle a home once more. He was to succeed in this – 'the new pirates of Halford Castle' he was to christen the Collingham family in the years to come. 'If you do decide to take it on, there's another point I'd like to go into,' was all he said then.

He came over now to meet Libby, bringing with him the Vice-Chancellor of the university. 'Come and meet this couple,' he had said to him. 'Richard Collingham and his wife. He's the young surgeon who was injured in the Euston rail crash. He had a broken back, and now he's confined to a wheelchair. He can't practise as a surgeon, of course, any longer. As I mentioned the other day, I'm rather hoping to land him as

Director of the Student Health Service.'

'Sounds an excellent plan, if you think we could get him.'

'I think so. Yes, I think so. He's a very old friend of my son-in-law – staying with him now, as a matter of fact. I think we should be able to inveigle him down here, if we go about it the right way.'

'You want me to come with you and do some inveigling at the moment? Eh?'

'That's the general idea.'

'Is that the wife? What a beautiful girl. She'd be an acquisition at university dinner tables. Yes, indeed.'

'Perhaps you'd better concentrate on inveigling her, then.'

'A pleasure.' The Vice-Chancellor was not only an extremely able man, but also a noticeably charming one, and he laid himself out to please Libby.

Sir John invited the whole group to dinner after the garden party. Richard accepted with alacrity, though Libby muttered to Catherine, 'Do you think I could escape and give Julie a hand with the children, and then come back here later? Or would it look frightfully rude?'

'No need,' Catherine said with confidence. 'Victoria can help her. She's very capable, though I admit you wouldn't think it to look at her now. She can take herself and all those feathers back to Harbour's Eye and look after Julie and the children.'

Libby was a little shattered. A day or two earlier she would not have believed it possible to find herself down at Halchester successfully dumping her children on Victoria while she calmly went to a dinner party with Richard.

Catherine, as deliberately as her father might have done, completed the healing process.

'Thank goodness,' she added, 'now that you're all here, Victoria's going to sleep at the Lawns. She won't appear until after breakfast to take Richard for his physio-therapy at St Mark's. He swears he can manage by himself until then. Adam says Richard's very restive under her over-cosseting, and wants his independence.'

'He never has cared for cherishing,' Libby agreed. 'I've often wished he took to it more. How we'll manage now I daren't think, because he'll have to have so much done for him, and he does loathe it so.'

'Adam says he'll accept it as long as you do it in a very matter-of-fact way.'

'Heather!' Libby ejaculated.

'M-mm?' Catherine looked around, slightly bewildered. No sign of the ubiquitous child.

'Heather's way. That's how she is. She's all Collingham. I'll have to watch her, and take lessons in handling him from her.'

Victoria accepted without question Libby's request that she should return to Harbour's Eye and help Julie to put the children to bed. She accomplished this with her usual efficiency, then drove herself back to the Lawns to her own comfortable bedroom for the first time. Lying in bed after her bath, she faced a bleak future. She loved Richard, yet she knew now that her own part was minor, a temporary expedient, no more. Her participation in his life was nearly over. Libby and the children had joined him at Harbour's Eye, and she was no more to them – or indeed, she knew bitterly to Richard himself – than the *au pair* girl, or the physiotherapist at St Mark's. She was faced with remaining to care for him, knowing herself of no account. Their relationship had been a game to him, of which he had now tired.

Here she was right. Richard had found her surprisingly attractive, and her competent sophistication showed him as clearly as it had Adam that there was no danger of unwelcome involvement. Normally he was wary of beautiful young girls. He had Libby at home, and at the hospital he played safe. But after his accident he was in a different mood. He was looking for reassurance, and when his body responded to Victoria's beauty he had encouraged the reaction, relieved and delighted to find any response still in him. He was, in fact, putting in a little practice, and would have been astounded to discover that this had in any way affected Libby, who should have known herself secure in his enduring love. This had nothing to do with her.

Victoria knew his. She had known it from the beginning. Good clean fun, she thought sourly, taken seriously by neither. An amusement she had been as expert in as he, which had been, after all, no more than a stage in his rehabilitation, had meant only that he was picking up the threads of life. She had gone into it with her eyes open. But it had been too much for her, and now she could not see how she was to go through the next few days. She must remain charming, attentive and apparently light-hearted, while she watched him turn to Libby.

She would throw the job up. Go to Vietnam. Nurses were needed there. She could forget herself nursing in the East, trying to salvage some of the human debris of war.

She lay for some time thinking about this. But above the image of herself in a stunning uniform, another picture rose. Richard, managing alone for the first time.

At this point she saw that it was not Vietnam for her, but Richard Collingham for the weeks or months – it could not be more – that he continued to need her. She would have to learn how to take a back seat.

She smiled involuntarily. Victoria, as Catherine had observed, was not the superficial kitten that she often liked to pretend. She knew that to take a back seat was not exactly her line. But it had to be done. 'You must write yourself out of this script,' she told herself. It was to be one of the most difficult achievements of her career, and no one was to give her any credit for it.

As she reached this decision, the Collinghams and the Trowbridges returned to a peacefully sleeping Harbour's Eye. Even Julie had gone to bed. Everything was neat and tidy. Victoria had been, as ever, efficient. There was nothing for Catherine or Libby to do. Libby looked in on the children, tucked Gavin in again, and smiled at Heather's watch put ready at the side of her bed as though she were a commuter catching an early train. Adam told her he would see Richard into bed, and she accepted this as being almost certainly what Richard would prefer. Afterwards, though, lonely in her room upstairs, she decided to take her first lesson from Heather. She would do what she wanted to do, unless stopped by major force. She went downstairs in her summer housecoat, her hair hanging on her shoulders, and into Richard's room.

He was lying on his back in bed, staring at the ceiling. 'Hullo,' he said, 'it's you. Shall I take that job?'

'This one here? The Student Health Service?'

'Yes.'

'You want to, don't you?'

'More than I do the other.'

'You take it, darling. It seems to me much more you than the Central job.'

'Probably is. All right, I will.' He said nothing for a moment or two, then turned his head suddenly and said, 'Adam had *Nocturne* brought round here. We went for a short sail.'

'What was it like?' Libby asked, trying hard to sound casual.

He gave her a sharp look. 'You sounded

just like Heather then. Extraordinary. It was all right.'

'Then if you take this job, you could sail her from here as well, with Adam.'

'Adam will be too busy most of the time. You'll be the one. You'll have to sail with me.'

'And Heather will learn.'

'Yes. I daresay she'll be quite good.'

'I daresay she will. If a bit overbearing.'

'She needs putting down with a heavy hand.'

'Poor lamb, she's only a bit bossy. And she is the eldest.'

Libby was sitting on the side of the bed, and they remained in companionable silence for a while. Libby looked at Richard. They were alone and uninterrupted at last. She put out her hand and pushed his hair back from his forehead, and smoothed his temples. He took her hand and held on to it. Their eyes met.

'I'm coming in to bed with you,' Libby said. She took off her housecoat.

He gave her a quick blank look, and stared at the ceiling again.

Libby's heart dropped. He didn't want her.

'It won't be any good,' he commented flatly, and shut his eyes with finality.

Libby looked at him in despair. She could not see how to deal with this. Momentarily she thought of Heather, but her daughter had no answers for her here. She watched Richard with love and tenderness, and suddenly she understood him again as she had always done in the past. He was not trying to repulse her. It was not that he didn't want her. He was afraid.

Her heart went out to him, and she heard herself speaking. 'Darling,' she was saying, 'I want to hold on to you. I've been so lonely without you all this time.'

His body was the comfort to her it had always been. She held him tightly and felt his response. He opened his eyes. They were alight with love and a dawning triumph.